I0521183

Ana
Ana of Austria (1568 – 1629)

an unfinished historical novel

Linda Carlino

VeritasPublishing
8 Vane Road Barnard Castle
County Durham DL12 8AQ
England

This paperback edition first published in 2011

Copyright © 2010 by Linda Carlino

The moral right of the author has been asserted.
All rights reserved. No part of this publication
may be reproduced or transmitted, in any form
or by any means, without the prior written
permission of the publisher.

Front cover photo: Museo del Prado (Madrid)
Back cover photo: Junta de Castilla y León

ISBN: 978-0-9555980-3-6

Printed and bound by
BookPrintingUK.com
Peterborough, England

www.VeritasPublishing.co.uk

also by Linda Carlino

A Spanish Hapsburg Trilogy:

That Other Juana
A Matter of Pride
Wives & Other Women

Brief Synopsis

Ana, known as Ana of Austria, was the illegitimate daughter of Juan de Austria, who was himself the illegitimate son of Charles V (HRE). She was raised by the same nanny as her father until she was seven then placed in a convent in Avila.

Later her confessor introduced her to the convent's young, handsome pastry chef, Gabriel de Espinosa. He claimed to be King Sebastian I of Portugal, who was never convincingly accounted for after a battle in Morocco. With the complicity of her confessor they started courting.

Espinosa bore a surprising resemblance to the missing king Sebastian and Ana was duped into believing his claim to the throne. And dazzled by his charm and the hope of becoming queen of Portugal, she fell in love with him and became involved in the complicated and dangerous political intrigue surrounding the Portuguese crown.

Historical Background

In late 16th century Portugal hopes of ending Spanish control of their country rested on the safe return of their king Sebastian from battle in Morocco. But he did not return. It was assumed, but never proved, that he was killed in battle. Remains, never positively identified, were returned and ceremoniously buried in the presence of King Philip II of Spain.

But many Portuguese refused to accept the authenticity of the remains and maintained that Sebastian was still alive and would eventually be found and returned to Portugal. And this hope was given support by Spain's enemies France and England.

This situation gave rise to many claimants to the Portuguese throne and, consequently, much intrigue, and many plots and counter-plots.

Acknowledgements

Many thanks to all my friends in Madrid without whose help and encouragement my books might never have been published, in particular: Antonio Machín García, Josep M. Sanmartí, and especially Miguel Ruiz-Borrego y Arabal, who's gift to me of El Pastelero de Madrigal by Manuel Fernádez y González, ignited my interest in the topic and led directly to my writing this book.

My thanks also to the Biblioteca Nacional and the Casino of Madrid for the use of their wonderful libraries and archives, and the British Library and the Durham County Library, especially the Barnard Castle branch, for all their help.

And my special thanks to our dear friend Lucía Alvarez de Toledo for her help and support over many years.

Chapter 1

A door opened. For just an instant a shaft of bright yellow light enfolding the silhouette of a cloaked figure was thrown across the darkness; some distant music and laughter tumbled along unseen corridors and out along the golden beam before the door closed as quickly as it had opened and darkness and silence reclaimed the courtyard.

Horses shuffled and stamped disturbed by the silent speeding figure, the billowing cloak scattering delicate snowflakes on their earthbound journey swishing aside any that had already settled on the ground.

A plain, black carriage bearing neither coat of arms nor gilded embellishments waited for her. How much better it was this way she thought; anonymity was wiser.

Two gentlemen stood by the carriage one bearing a lantern the other ready to gather her up into his arms to kiss her, to lift her and her trailing skirts into the cocoon of padded velvet. He clambered in behind her and swiftly helped wrap her in luxurious fur rugs. They pressed their feet against a foot warmer and the door was slammed shut against the freezing January night; northern Spain was always bitterly cold in winter. The coachman hissed his order and they were on their way.

'How dared I even contemplate this? I can scarcely breathe, my heart is pounding, my head spinning. Is it true, dare I believe?'

'Oh, my Ana,' she was drawn close and lips gently kissed once, twice, three times. 'We are not dreaming; that is real.'

The rich timbre of his voice was exactly the same as it had been those many years ago, its dark tones and faint accent still capable of sending waves of excitement through her.

She leaned towards the window, to whisper her farewells: to King Philip's carriage standing alone and aloof, to the pilgrims' hospital, the Chapel of Santiago, the Chapel of San Juan, the sightless walls of the cloister, to the convent's arched gateway.

They were out on the highway, 'I am free! Goodbye Las Huelgas, and goodbye Burgos!' she called out into the night before returning to the arms of her beloved. 'I am free and I have you at my side,' her hand caressed his short trimmed grey beard.

Moments later she asked, 'Do you suppose the snow will amount to much?'

He answered whispering across her cheek, 'I dare say that would be convenient. The roads are frozen hard and even a light covering would soon hide our tracks.'

'I wonder what will be said when they discover my absence?'

'Very little, my dear, and even that would be behind closed doors and only in very hushed voices. No one will want it made public knowledge. But what they think or say is of no interest to me. From this moment my thoughts are for you and you alone. First I need to get you to Seville where the Andalucían sun will melt the northern chill from our bones. Then, when the time is right for you we will go to Naples. I so want you to see our new home, but I can wait, I am a patient man.'

'But we cannot travel to Seville tonight,' she felt a moment's alarm, 'neither of us is young enough to be embarking on ...'

'Do not worry your pretty little head. I have arranged several halts on our journey. We shall stay with friends, for years all sympathisers and supporters. Each and every one is impatient to meet and welcome my darling wife.' He sought her hands beneath the rugs, 'At last we two can live as one.'

She laughed, pulling her hands free to burrow in a deep pocket of her robe, 'We three can live as one.'

'Good Lord, the doll!' He took the weary-looking toy, almost too afraid to touch the faded gown with its still intact garlands of beads. 'Our accomplice; and a remarkably successful one at that. How could we possibly go anywhere without her?'

'Maria has been my friend for years, too many to count; my only friend at times.'

'I insist she promises never to remind you of those dark days. Rest now.'

Ana nestled her head against his breast. He brought the rug up over her shoulders. The carriage jerked and jolted over the rutted roads carrying them to their new life.

Her eyes closed. She was happy at last and able to remember the past without any pain, seeing it as no more than a lengthy prelude.

And so she allowed the days and years to unfold telling a story, their story the strangest of stories.

Chapter 2

Six years old Ana was on her floor cushion in the large salon sewing. Her needle poked in and out and along the hem of a white piece of cloth perhaps destined to be a handkerchief or even a napkin.

She was hot, her hands were sticky, and the needle squeaked its begrudging way followed by a no longer white length of thread leaving a trail of uneven stitches. All she wanted was to be with her friends, to play the promised game of dressing their dolls.

Fortunately snippets of conversation between her Lady Aunt Magdalena and the visiting priest did, at least, provide some diversion, and nurse had to tug at Ana's sleeve more than once to direct her attention back to her sewing.

'Yes,' Doña Magdalena continued, 'the problems in the Low Countries continue, and his majesty has decided that Don Juan should be in command, to bring the heretics to their knees.'

'When does he sail?'

Magdalena lowered her voice, 'Everyone assumes my nephew is going by sea, but he had no intention of waiting for favourable tides or winds, deciding instead to travel overland. He came here to say farewell and also to change his appearance. We dyed those beautiful blond curls black and stained his face and hands.'

Ana stopped sewing.

The priest was curious. 'So that he would look like a Moor?'

Ana so wished she could have been present at such a marvellous game.

'Yes, Brother Goldáraz; a Moor. He made himself resemble one of those hateful creatures who killed his uncle, my beloved husband.'

Ana pictured that kind old uncle who was now lying in his tomb in the family chapel; she had seen him only occasionally, but she remembered how he never forgot to tousle her head whenever he visited.

'And off he went as his friend's servant, the pair of them galloping across Spain and France, and no one apparently any the wiser. And yet I am convinced there would be many to say *under this common outfit we have a prince.*'

'Ana,' whispered her nurse, 'back to your sewing young lady.'

Brother Goldáraz smiled and nodded, 'You must be very proud of His Excellency Don Juan.'

'Of course; he is courageous, an excellent leader; but it does not free him from his sins.'

'We are none of us free from sin, dear lady, but he cannot be held responsible for his begetters.'

'So you say, but I am not entirely convinced of that. He is tainted by the same weaknesses. Dear Lord but the world is such a very wicked place. The weakness of the flesh is the undoing of so many, and it leaves others to deal with its consequences.'

'A great concern of yours, my lady, and you have always shown great Christian charity, a champion of so many who have fallen.'

'Quite so; have you counted the money?'

'Six hundred *ducados*; the prioress cannot fail to be delighted with your beneficence. It is waiting to be stored in the carriage.'

Ana's needle stopped again, her eyes as wide as wide could be. Six hundred *ducados*; that was an enormous amount of money! You could buy all sorts with that; she had seen how much the poor could buy with the tiny *reales* her Lady Aunt gave them at Christmastide, and those were just a tiny fraction of a *ducado*.

'And the papers, Brother?'

'I have them here. You can see they have now been signed by all parties, including the lawyer on behalf of the king.'

Doña Magdalena de Ulloa studied the documents and their seals, to ensure that everything was in order. As she raised her eyes she noticed Ana. 'Put your sewing away, you may go down to the courtyard to play with your friends until the arrival of the condessa. You are to accompany her; nurse will let you know when it is time for you to prepare for your journey.'

Of all the things she had heard this afternoon this was the most unexpected and the most exciting. At long last she was going to stay with this aunt. Today she was leaving Villagarcía to travel with the Condessa de Salinas. The condessa was very rich and lived in an enormous palace, and if they weren't going there then they would be going to Madrid because she was one of Queen Anne's ladies.

Ana could not believe her good fortune. The condessa was completely different in every way imaginable to Lady Aunt Magdalena: she wore such beautiful clothes instead of her Lady Aunt's black, always black, even before uncle died; she was always cheerful, smiling and laughing, never stern or solemn. This was going to be enormous fun!

Her needlework was thrust aside, Maria her doll and a basket of dolls' clothes hastily snatched up, a hurried curtsey, and she was off. There was the game to look forward to, of course, but she had so much to tell.

The courtyard was dazzling white in the July sun. She scampered across the flagstones eager to be in the shade with her playmates.

'We thought you weren't coming,' said one.

'We thought you'd forgotten,' said the other.

'I had to do my sewing,' Ana panted. 'But, listen to my good news; I am going on holiday with the Condessa de Salinas. She is coming to collect me today.'

'Is she the rich lady?'

'Yes, and I might be going to Madrid. Let's dress our dolls for a ball in Madrid.'

The basket was searched for skirts, bodices, panels, gowns, for miniature necklaces and ropes of glass beads. So many were selected, to be discarded or swapped until the little girls were satisfied with the finished results; then the whole process begun all over again, and again, with undiminished intensity.

'Ana,' nurse had arrived, 'you must come now.'

Dolls were dropped into laps. This had never happened before; Ana was going away, she wouldn't be joining in their games for a while.

'I'll have lots to tell you when I return. I expect I will be too busy to play very much with my doll, so you may keep the basket of clothes. Promise to take care of them. Will you come to wave me goodbye?' Without waiting for any replies Ana skipped off with nurse.

In her bedchamber Ana was undressed, her hands and face given a thorough washing – nurse could be so rough at times — and Ana had to keep her eyes tight shut and her lips quite sealed against the fierce attack of face cloth and towel. A fresh chemise was slipped over her head, a petticoat tied at her waist and she was ready to put on her new dress.

She was bitterly disappointed; it was black, made from the remnants of her Lady Aunt's latest gown!

Nurse was swift to explain, 'Doña Magdalena prefers you wear something suitable for the journey and the material was available, you know how your Lady Aunt hates waste. Your other dresses are in your trunk. Now for your hair.'

Nurse ran the brush through the long golden curls then the silken locks were carefully braided. Tears tumbled over nurse's cheeks. 'I shall miss doing this,' she sniffed.

Ana turned to hug the one who was always as warm and comforting as her ample bosom, 'And I shall miss you. But I shall be away for only a short while, and you can enjoy having the bed all to yourself, without me to trouble you with my toothaches or coughs.'

'Get away with you, you can never be any trouble,' she cupped the small pretty face with her hands. Two huge blue eyes looked up at her, and the tiny rosebud mouth widened into a smile. Nurse cleared her throat, 'Now let's not get silly; Doña Magdalena will be waiting.'

The condessa was there looking just as exquisite as Ana had expected; a beautiful shimmer of blue satins and twinkling gems. Ana joined her and the priest in the carriage after a frantic last-minute dash back to her room to rescue her doll.

The farewells were over. These had been brief: her Lady Aunt's more of an admonishment to be good; her nurse's hug, strong enough to squeeze the very breath out of her; her little friends' gauche waves.

The coach jerked and lurched forward leaving the courtyard, followed by a van of luggage carts.

Ana was on her way. She kneaded the padded velvet seat between her fingers, rested back against the soft cushions. The condessa's dress was now covered by a plain, long sleeved linen gown to protect it from the inevitable dust kicked up by the horses' hooves and wheels; dust that the carriage curtains couldn't possibly prevent from finding its way onto the passengers.

It seemed the condessa and the priest had little to say to one another and Ana knew it would be considered an impertinence for her to speak. The creaking, groaning, clattering progress went on for hours with only the occasional commands from the impatient coachman to break the monotony.

Eventually the wheel sounds changed and the shadows of buildings darkened the carriage. The condessa drew aside a window covering.

'Ah, at last, Madrigal de las Altas Torres.'

Ana was surprised that the condessa's voice should be tinged with impatience; it was usually light and jolly. She supposed it was due to the tiresome journey.

The two adults and Ana entered the comparative cool of the entrance lobby, the priest rang a bell, and they waited.

Chapter 3

On the other side of a door just as big and as strong as the one they had passed through leading from the street the bell could be heard calling out for attention.

As they waited the servants carried in the chest of *ducados* and rested it on the stone bench normally used by visitors waiting for someone to receive them. The condessa flapped at the air with her fan; the priest adjusted his robes and scapula; Ana gazed at the walls, bare except for a huge but plain wooden cross and the little wooden window, exactly the same as the one at Villagarcía, where a nun would eventually appear to ask what you wanted.

A key rattled in the lock and the door was pulled open by a cadaverous and mean-looking nun in a black habit, the enormous key on an equally large key ring on its heavy chain looking every bit as important as the rosary hanging from her belt. This was Sister Leonor, the keeper of the key.

'Condessa, welcome to the Royal Convent of Our Lady of Grace. Brother Goldáraz, welcome. The prioress is ready to receive you.' She called over her shoulder, 'Sister Isabel.'

Goldáraz muttered his greeting, 'Sister Leonor,' keeping his eyes averted; there was something about this woman he could never like, try as he might.

A second nun appeared, Sister Isabel, as jolly and plump as could be.

'Sister Isabel, will you look after Ana for a few moments?'

Isabel shot her a questioning look then held out her hand to welcome the child. 'Hello Ana; Do you think a little walk would be lovely after so long a ride, yes? Shall we go then?'

As they walked in the cloister Ana asked, 'How did you know my name?'

The nun smiled down at her, 'There is no mystery; the prioress told us.'

'I am travelling with the condessa because I am going to stay with her for a while.'

'Are you now; and I see you have your doll as companion.'

Ana held up her toy, 'This is Maria, she goes everywhere with me. Your convent is much grander than the one we have in Villagarcía; my Lady Aunt Magdalena takes me there often, so I know.'

Sister Isabel chuckled at the serious child at her side, 'This is much grander than most. Some very important people have lived or stayed here; in fact a princess was born here.'

'A princess, born here and not in a palace? Princesses are always born in palaces; at least they are in nurse's stories.'

'Nurse is more or less right, this convent was actually part palace and that is why a princess was born here. She grew up to be our queen, Queen Isabel the Catholic. A little later I shall take you to the bedchamber where she came into the world.'

But Ana was anxious, 'May I go now because I think we might be setting off soon?'

'We still have lots of time. Shall we visit the orchard to gather some fruit?'

The idea was sorely tempting, but, 'The condessa will not know where I am.'

'Have no fears little one. You will be quite safe with me.' Sister Isabel swallowed hard, she had to follow orders.

In the orchard Ana swiftly chose three apples and three pears, enough she insisted for the three travellers, 'I think we should go back to the cloister to wait.'

'What about playing at throwing an apple to each other? Let me find one shaped like a ball.'

Ana tugged at the nun's skirts, 'We have to get back to the cloister or I might miss the condessa.'

'Come along then.'

They sat on a stone seat both listening, watching, as doors opened and shut, but they only saw nuns going about their business.

'Tell me about your doll.' The nun's fingers traced along the threaded beads, stroked the satin sleeves.

'She is going to a ball. She has lots of other clothes. I left them with my friends to play with while I am away. But I don't want to talk about that now; I want to go with the condessa. Will you take me to the room of the lady prioress?'

'I truly cannot do that unless I am summoned.'

Sister Leonor appeared and Ana raced across the cloister, Sister Isabel doing her utmost to hurry her plump self after.

Leonor thrust Ana to one side as she unlocked the door, disappeared for a moment then returned. She turned the key once more, and it made the most terrible grating noise in that awful lock. 'Everything is secure for the night. We can now all go to our rooms.'

Ana was bewildered, 'Where is the condessa?'

Leonor looked down her thin nose and gave Ana one of her most withering of withering looks. She had no time for these little rich girls, nuisances all of them, upsetting the routine of the community even if they did bring in a substantial portion of the convent's income. 'The condessa left a while ago.'

'You are wrong; I am waiting for her!'

'Guard your tongue rude child! Sister Isabel, have you not told her? Dear Lord in Heaven, you are so weak. So it is left to me.' She fixed Ana with an icy stare, 'Ana de Jesus, as from today this is your home. You have come here to serve God.'

Ana screamed, she pummelled at the lock, kicked at the door, tugged at the key on its ring amongst the folds of Sister Leonor's robes, 'Let me go, I hate it here; I want to go with the condessa. You must have tricked her, told her I'd gone then you locked the door!'

'Sister Isabel, tell this ill-tempered infant that she has commenced her novitiate and there is nothing more to be said on the matter.'

'Sister Leonor, have you forgotten the milk of human kindness?'

'One has to be cruel to be kind.' She prized the key free from Ana's desperate fingers and walked briskly away.

'She's lying, she's lying,' Ana sobbed.

Isabel knelt down to gather the child in her arms. 'What Sister Leonor says is true. Your Aunt, Doña Magdalena de Ulloa, and His Highness King Philip II have decided you should become an Augustinian nun. Evidently you are destined one day to become an abbess. My poor, sweet child there is no mistake; I was present when the papers were signed. I can only hope you will forgive me for my part in today's deception. I will do everything I can to atone for my sins.'

Ana had heard nothing from behind her wall of choking sobs, where she reeled in fear.

Chapter 4

Isabel carried the still sobbing child up the stone stairs, along the gallery then set her down.

'These are your apartments, shall you open the door? No? Then I shall do it.'

A reluctant Ana was gently nudged into a salon. The floor was terracotta tiled but at the far end there was a carpeted wooden dais with several floor cushions, in fact the whole room was decorated in the style required for a lady of noble birth. Two windows opened out into the gallery and a further two, ridiculously high, faced the town square.

Isabel ushered Ana first to the kitchen, then into the small private chapel, followed by a brief look into a retiring room, and finally into the bedchamber. Ana's howls were louder than ever the moment she saw the bed. It was the same size as the sanctuary she shared with her nurse at Villagarcía.

'My nurse,' she wailed, 'I want my nurse. Please tell them to bring my nurse.' She grasped Isabel's skirts, burying her wet cheeks and chin into the woollen folds.

'I will be your nurse. I will be all the things your nurse was, and more,' she stroked the golden head, wondering what to say next; what could she say? 'I shall tell you about these apartments. This is the bedchamber where Queen Isabel was born.'

Ana was only half listening but Isabel's words helped disrupt the ever-growing panic determined to overwhelm her.

'Queen Isabel was born a long, long, time ago. After a few years later she moved from here to live with her mother and tiny baby brother in a castle. In fact the little family were locked away in the castle by their wicked half-brother, the king. He was very unkind to them, often leaving them without food or money. One day, when she was quite grown up this half-brother said she had to marry a marqués. This marqués was as evil as the king himself. He came to stay here on his way to marry Isabel, and while he was here he got very sick and died, right here in this convent! Some people said that Isabel's best friend poisoned him. Then Isabel heard about this handsome prince called Ferdinand and she decided to marry him, no matter what her half-brother thought. And so she did, in secret. When the wicked half-brother died they became king and queen and lived happily ever after. There now, did you like that story?'

There was no answer, but at least Ana had finally stopped crying.

Isabel led Ana back to the salon. She hurried about the room gathering dishes and setting the table. 'You may not feel hungry but your servants have prepared some special treats for you and I spent an age squeezing oranges to make you some juice.'

They sat together picking and pecking at various dishes, Sister Isabel watching over her ward, rejoicing at every morsel swallowed.

Later, when they were both in their nightshifts and tucked up in the great bed Ana snuggled next to her new 'nurse' to ask for another story.

'This is about Maria, your doll, who is really a princess. Maria lived in a palace, and she always wanted to go to a ball.'

Ana propped her doll between them then put a comforting thumb in her mouth her fingers curled about her nose.

'The king and queen always said no. They made lots of excuses: first it was because she was too young, then she didn't know the steps, then there were no princes in the land to invite and they would only allow her to dance with a prince.'

'Nurse only tells me happy stories,' Ana stopped sucking her thumb for a moment.

'Be patient a while. One day a prince from a neighbouring country learned about the unhappy princess and came riding into the country.'

'Did he come with his army?' Ana mumbled around her thumb.

'Not a bit of it; he and a few friends came disguised as merchants. They said they had brought fine materials to show the princess. But as soon as Princess Maria saw the prince she fell in love with him.'

'And did they go to the ball?'

'No, they escaped and galloped away as fast as they could to the prince's country where ...'

'Where they lived happily ever after.'

Ana finally drifted into sleep, Isabel kissed the golden head whispering, 'Who knows, one day your own prince may come to rescue you. Do fairy tales come true? I doubt it, but it can be fun dreaming.'

Chapter 5

The audience chamber in Lisbon's royal palace, the Paco da Ribera, was crowded. Business was over for the day but many lingered; after all large sums of money had been spent on finery in the hope that their wearers would be recognised by someone of influence.

The young king of Portugal, King Sebastian, had had enough of the crush, the noise, the heat. From his throne on the dais he motioned with impatience to his great uncle, cardinal and regent, to dismiss the throng.

Cardinal Enrique staggered to his feet, nodded in the direction of the doormen. The doors were opened and the red velvets and satins the gold silks and damasks flowed out and away like a stream caught in glorious sunset. The portraits lining the walls, all of past monarchs in their full regalia, appeared but a poor imitation of the luxury that passed beneath them.

The twenty years old sovereign, his grandmother Queen Catalina, and great uncle Enrique remained, marooned in the vast emptiness; alone except for Sebastian's two constant companions in their black robes who waited in silence at the doorway.

'It truly is quite insufferable having to receive so many people at once!' Sebastian slammed his hands against the gilded arms of the throne. He strode over to the windows to throw one open.

Catalina's eyes followed the blond haired youth, a disappointing monarch totally disinterested in royal duties, any royal duties. It was a blessing that the cardinal was at hand to be of help. However, and this worried many, Portugal was a rich and powerful nation and she needed more than a sickly priest on his sixties at her helm.

Sebastian gazed down at the ships anchored in the harbour and sighed his ongoing frustration. He returned to his former proud and arrogant self to face his family, the last of his closest kin, those two elderly beings sitting as immobile as if they were already effigies on their tombstones.

'Who was my father?' he demanded.

'What nonsense is this?' Catalina was caught completely off guard. She shook her head in disbelief, her cascade of chins tumbling down to her more than ample breast. 'You grow more annoying by the day. You know full well your dear father was heir to the throne.'

'Of course I know that,' he snapped irritably. He gestured towards the portrait of Prince John, his father, 'But who was he, what was the man like? I tell you he was not much of a man.'

'Sebastian how could you, you go too far! Cardinal would you please say something?' The quivering chins were now purple.

'You are being quite tiresome. You know full well your father's life was cruelly cut short. He was a young man who had rarely enjoyed good health.'

Catalina dabbed a handkerchief to her eyes, her nose, then settled it on her lips, 'My poor darling was ill so often.'

Sebastian began to strut about the room emphasising his own superior strength. The entire court was aware that no one could match him at swimming and fencing, that his arms and legs could quiet the most spirited of horses.

Catalina continued, 'And let us not forget that you too were very sickly as a child. You were partially lame ... your leg ...'

He silenced her, 'And look at me; no weak child now! Through my own rigorous efforts I conquered my weak body, made it a robust physical monument, whereas my father submitted to infirmity.'

He unsheathed his sword and cut several swathes in the air striding towards her. He stopped, took the blade in his hands and held it hilt upwards like a processional cross.

'Lest you be in any doubt, I am physically and morally strong enough to lead a Portuguese army, God's army. I will show that dead father, your son of such happy memories, and the two of you, that I am of sterner mettle.'

The cardinal did not disguise his annoyance with this boy king who had never shown the slightest interest in Portugal's affairs, who chose instead either to practise his physical skills or, and this was much to his consternation, to escape his royal duties to spend hours in the company of those two monks discussing the writings of Saint Thomas Aquinas.

'The prince, your father was a victim of consumption which daily attacked his delicate frame, finally destroying him; but not, thank God, before he had seen your safe arrival into this world. As your grandmother says, we all praise God for bringing you through those dark days of your own childhood when you were often seriously ill; and I might add that your survival was in great part due to your grandmother's choice of doctors.'

Sebastian angrily thrust his sword back into its scabbard, 'Doctors; I have done with their meddling! Perhaps if my mother had stayed she could have prevented them from all their prying and poking, forever embarrassing me ... but ...'

'Princess Juana had to return to Spain to act as regent.'

'No matter, we are losing the point. You appear to have ignored my momentous announcement. I am preparing to lead an army, a crusade against the infidel in Morocco. I shall continue the work of my grandfather, the Holy Roman Emperor Charles V.' He waited in the silence, but not for too long, 'Does that not make you feel proud to have such a grandson? And you, cardinal, you must have something to say, surely?'

The cardinal's response was blunt, 'A remarkable challenge considering you spend your time preferring to hide from unwelcome visitors, avoiding royal council meetings whenever possible, tiptoeing about the palace with those two excuses for priests.'

Sebastian's pale and freckled face reddened, 'How dare you sir!'

'I dare because I am regent. If, however, you are being serious and not just seeking to shock then let me say I am concerned for our country and what will become of her if you insist on such an idiotic enterprise.'

Catalina sought to diffuse the situation; she found these family squabbles very difficult to bear. 'Grandson; you are to be congratulated for your dedication to the Faith. I applaud your reformation of the religious military orders, it demonstrates your commitment. I am impressed with your dedication to train your body. Have no doubt I will support your crusade wholeheartedly once you have provided Portugal with an heir.'

Cardinal Enrique continued the theme, 'Indeed, my lady. Sebastian you must consider this: Spain would be only too ready to pounce if you go and there were to be a – a fatality. Yes, if Portugal has no heir she will be swallowed whole by King Philip and his Spain.'

'You wrong Uncle Philip greatly. I can show you his letter where he vows that during my absence he will guard Portugal against all possible enemies, including adventurous Castilians.'

'You are wrong' the cardinal wheezed, 'I may be a cynic, but Philip's words are hinting already at invasion. May I also suggest to you that he appears to me as the mature and experienced monarch seeking to encourage a young and totally naïve monarch to take a path to total ruin in order to suit his own purposes.'

'Great uncle you are indeed a cynic. We shall see just how wrong you are when I visit my uncle in Spain in December to discuss his possible aid and support. Everything has been arranged. Enough; these are my final words: I have every intention of going to Morocco, to annihilate the infidel. Never fear, grandmother, on my return I shall marry and provide heirs. Meanwhile great uncle you will continue as regent. I have spoken and there is no more to be said.' He clapped his hands, calling to the monks, 'Have those fellows come in now.'

A table was carried into the room and stood at the centre and, with great reverence, a velvet covered box placed on it.

Sebastian fell to his knees in prayer. The velvet cover was withdrawn to reveal a glass reliquary. 'This proves the earnestness of my intent. Here before you is a most precious gift from His Holiness the Pope. With its aid there can be no fear of any defeat, God will be on our side.'

Cardinal Enrique assisted Catalina in her unsteady walk towards the holy relic.

The young king proudly announced, 'This is one of the original arrows that killed the martyr Saint Sebastian.

The elderly pair crossed themselves.

Chapter 6

Ana was determined to make it her very best writing, her tongue echoing every curve and stroke in the words that Sister Leonor, the *key lady*, dictated. It was by now a regular routine, the bony fingers of the nun tracing across the paper intimidating an already insecure child.

Two years had passed and Ana's only contact, if it could be called contact, with the Lady Aunt Magdalena was through these letters that the prioress insisted she write; letters of gratitude for the gifts of money for her food, her clothing, her servants — none of which she would have needed had she been allowed to remain at home she told herself — letters to an aunt who never replied or came to visit her. She had written letters of her own, written with the help of Sister Isabel, but there was never a response.

The pen was set down. The child's scrawl was given a final inspection.

'I suppose it will do,' Sister Leonor was singularly unimpressed. 'I shall take it to the prioress for posting. Sister Isabel, make these children presentable. When they are ready conduct them to the *locutorio*, the visitors' room, they have a visitor.' She muttered angrily to herself as she left, 'Servants, fancy food, visitors; whatever next.'

Ana and her two friends, who had been patiently waiting while she completed her task, squealed, took hands and skipped in a ring; a visitor!

'It is probably our brother come to bring more family news!'

Ana looked forward to seeing Blas just as much as the others; as she had no family of her own theirs had become hers and she loved to hear everything he had to say.

Louisa and Maria had been the one bright ray of sunshine in a grim, sad world. Two little girls, the same age as Ana. They had come from a family grown too large to keep. It had been their lot to be packed off to a convent. This was nothing unusual, it was the case in many a family of gentlefolk. They were girls, and girls were a strain on the purse strings. Families could only afford so much for dowries and those without were unmarriageable and therefore would have to remain at home to be fed and clothed, a financial impossibility.

The Lady Aunt Magdalena had heard of the father's decision and in a rare moment of benevolence towards Ana offered to support the children, allowing them to live in Ana's apartments until they were sixteen years old and ready to start their novitiate. They shared her lessons in reading, writing, arithmetic, and a not too rigorous study of Latin. They also slept together in the big bed where they could snuggle together to share their tears and laughter.

Sister Isabel benefited too, a small truckle bed had been placed at its foot allowing her the luxury of sleeping alone. She loved her little charges dearly but there was nothing like some privacy at the end of the day.

'Hands and faces first, then hair.'

They stood in line dutifully waiting their turn.

Ana asked, 'Do you suppose Brother Goldáraz would carry a letter for me?'

'Whatever made you think of such a thing?'

'I wondered if, somehow, you could smuggle one to him and he could hide it in his robes and then he could take it to Villagarcía, he is always going there. I think Sister Leonor is so spiteful that she has always destroyed those that I thought she would take to the prioress for me.'

Isabel tut-tutted, 'It is wrong of you to speak so ill of someone.'

'But she is spiteful and horrid,' Louis and Maria chimed.

'Shame on you all!'

Her chidings were always done so gently, it was impossible for her to look or sound harsh, yet the girls always knew when they had been scolded.

'Sorry, Sister Isabel.'

'The sad fact is that it would be unwise to send a letter with Brother Goldáraz, it might cause trouble. Priests are often searched. In these wicked days so many priests are spies, or are spies disguised as priests. Doña Magdalena and His Majesty King Philip have decided you must live here and should Brother Goldáraz be discovered

35

carrying your letter of complaint; why, he would be put in prison without a doubt.'

'Priests are spies!' Ana was jubilant; it would make such a wonderful bedtime story. 'More; tell us more!'

'Not when we have to get ourselves downstairs. One final check; good, we can go.'

Isabel ushered her wards down the stairs, along the short distance of the cloister, and into the dimly lit *locutorio*. She arranged them in line near the latticed grille that divided the room to make the visitors' area quite separate.

A beautiful and very rich-looking lady entered, the jewels on her green velvets sparkling, defying the gloom, rejoicing in the merest hint of light from the few candles that were allowed. A fur-lined velvet cloak lay nonchalantly over her shoulders.

A servant placed a large wicker basket at the feet of her mistress then helped arrange her and her skirts and cloak in the visitors' chair.

Luisa and Maria exchanged glances; it was not their brother after all, but who could it be?

Ana knew exactly who it was. This was the Duquesa de Salinas; come to do what? For one brief but exquisite moment she believed that the duquesa had come to take her away. No, she knew it could not be. She held Luisa's hand and whispered the visitor's name.

The beautiful lady waved aside their greeting, impatient to speak. 'The Court having enjoyed the Christmas festivities in Guadalupe has now returned to Madrid. I have been given permission to spend some time visiting my home and family. Doña Magdalena and I thought that as I was in the vicinity it would be a splendid idea for me to bring you some votive candles.' She peered into the gloom seeking out the nun, 'Sister Isabel, I understand that is your name, you will be responsible for them, and to ensure the children keep them carefully attended.'

Had Ana truly dared to hope for a release from her prison, that hope was well and truly quashed – votive candles!

'Two votive candles are to be kept burning, one for King Philip's armies in the Netherlands and one for King Sebastian of Portugal and his army in Morocco. Oh, children, do come closer to the grille it is too aggravating having to raise my voice.'

Sister Isabel gently nudged the girls into line next to the iron lattice work.

'I shall tell you all about King Sebastian. While we were in Guadalupe he came there to beg a favour of King Philip. You must believe me when I say the king of Portugal is such a handsome young man looking quite magnificent wearing either red and gold or white and gold, his favourite colours. He prefers the high-collared jerkin, a jerkin beautifully pinked and braided, I might add, with just a show of a collar of Brussels lace. Our queen gave him a gift of a dozen or more lace-collared shirts, the workmanship quite extraordinary. The panes of his trunk hose were either edged with gold braid or pearls and gems. His bonnets were of velvet with pretty jewelled designs around the brim, and of course always with a feather. He was a delight for the eyes … yes … well … I suppose it might be difficult for you to visualise. King Sebastian looks so very like his mother, our late and much lamented Princess Juana. He has the fairest of complexions and hair as blond as blond can be, just like hers.'

She stopped to sigh and shake her head. She checked that she still had her little audience's attention. 'I am afraid that it is there that all similarity ends. He has the most dreadful of tempers; obviously lacked discipline when he was young. He flew into quite a rage when our king said he was unable to offer military help for his crusade. Can you picture it, an ill-tempered youth storming about the royal apartments brandishing his sword? I can tell you there were several who were most upset and many afraid. That is no way for anyone to behave, and certainly not when everyone had been so generous and kind to him since his arrival in Spain. I marvel at the rudeness of the youth of today.'

Ana had not been particularly interested in how he dressed or what sort of temper he had, especially when she hadn't even heard of him until today, but the image of a royal person, whether king or prince, charging in and out of rooms and along corridors sword in hand, now that was an entirely different matter. Here was a hero bent on rescuing a captive princess, a fairy tale in the making.

The visitor pressed on, 'I heard it said that King Sebastian actually had the effrontery to accuse our king of cowardice, afraid to face the infidel!'

Ana gawped, gazed round-eyed with amazement, wondering if King Philip would insist on having his head chopped off. Another story lay waiting there for sure.

'King Sebastian has left for Portugal to prepare his armies for war. King Philip placated him somewhat with the offer of a few ships and, what is more, he has promised King Sebastian the hand of Princess Isabel Clara Eugenia when he returns from Morocco.'

The children would have loved to hear more, this was the very stuff of stories: a king riding off into battle, killing the enemy, returning as a conquering hero, marrying a beautiful princess, everyone living happily ever after. It was of no consequence that in reality Princess Isabel was just their age and still far too young to be married.

'So, children, a candle is to be kept burning for the safety of King Sebastian and the success of his valiant Christian soldiers. The other candle is for King Philip's armies in the Netherlands who are fighting the rebels. The soldiers are most fortunate in having His Excellency Don Juan as their commander, a quite invincible leader, nevertheless ...'

Ana remembered him. He always called the Lady Aunt Magdalena *dearest aunt*. She was always happy when he was near; well, he was such a jolly sort of person. He was tall with blond hair; at least it was blond until his *dearest aunt* dyed it for him. He was the hero of Lepanto and lots of flags from the defeated enemy's ships hung in the church at Villagarcía. There was a piece of the Holy Cross there too, a gift from the Pope. Perhaps Don Juan would marry a princess when he returned from his battles.

'... and you must say daily prayers for both leaders.'

Ana, Louise, and Maria curtsied and promised they would. The visitor stood to bid them goodbye and she was gone.

Everything was as it had been before, nothing had changed, but at least they had some good ideas to make up new and very different bedtime stories.

Chapter 7

The heat of the North African August sun was long gone. It was night and it was cold, bitterly cold. Two men lay together amongst hundreds of dead. Grit and sand blew into their half-closed eyes, into their noses and mouths.

One of the men groaned. Immediately a hand was clamped firm against his lips holding them shut.

The hand's owner shifted his position whispering, 'Keep your voice low till I can be sure. Thank God you are alive; I thought I had lost you.'

'Who are you? Where are we?' the other's voice rasped. The hazy starlit world ebbed and flowed as he tried to focus beyond the searing pains in his head. There were more in his arm and hand but they were as nothing compared with those in his head. 'Water, I must have water.'

'Not yet. I have to be absolutely certain the scavengers have all gone.'

'Dear God; I beg you, get me water.'

Scavengers, the excruciating pains, lying here in the cold sandy night unable to move because of some incredible weight crushing his body; there was no sense to it and he was too ill to think.

Time passed, an interminably thirsty and agonising time, and then water, the longed-for nectar was on his cracked lips, spilling into his mouth. 'If I could sit up it would be better.'

'Can you? Let me move these.'

Whatever the weight was on his back was gradually heaved aside. The unknown comrade dragged him by his shoulders into his lap, and stream of cold water was poured into his welcoming mouth flowing into a throat as dry and gravelled as the desert. He winced when it was poured across his head wounds to swill them clean of sand and dirt and would have cried out except for the hand that slapped itself once more over his mouth.

'I beg your pardon, your majesty. I think we are safe, the damned infidels seem to have left with their booty, but it would be best not to draw attention to ourselves.'

'Infidels? Who the devil are you?'

'Cristobal da Silva; at your service your majesty, here to do whatever I can to keep you alive and get you to safety.'

'What are you saying?'

'When you come to your senses you will remember you are King Sebastian. I saw you fall under the blows of the enemies' swords and threw myself over you to protect you. As soon as I could I dragged other bodies, those poor devils I have just pulled out of the way, to cover us, bury us, if you like.'

'You call me a king?'

'King Sebastian of Portugal.'

A wind blew across them hurling a hail of sand into the newly cleansed gashes. Cristobal raised his cloak against the onslaught.

'This is a godforsaken place to find oneself, what are we doing here?'

'Sire, we are in Morocco, at Alcazarquivir. There was a battle; a hopeless, lost cause if ever there was one. The upshot is most of our men are dead, thousands of them too by my reckoning. It was simple enough, the enemy made an arc as if they were welcoming arms and we walked right in.'

'Which fool sent so many to their deaths?'

There was an awkward silence so the question was repeated demanding an answer.

'With respect, sire, it was the command of King Sebastian.'

'And you believe me to be him. I hope to God I am not; such shame, such guilt. I would never dare show my face again, could never bear to have anyone discover who I was. To carry so many deaths on one's conscience; I surely cannot be that man. But if I am, how could I ever be absolved of such a crime?'

'I cannot answer any of that. What I do know is that you are the king because I took the royal ring from your finger and several other jewels and, of course, the gold-plated armour you were wearing. I had to prevent the enemy from identifying you as they went about their business of looting; they can have a very swift and uncivilised method of removing rings and the like.'

Cristobal unsheathed his dagger to dig and scrape in the sand to retrieve a leather pouch, 'And here it is.' He slipped the thongs around his neck and dropped the pouch under his chemise. 'I am going for more water; we can have that and a bit of stale bread before we get on our way to the fort at Alcira. A few prayers might come in handy, asking God to persuade the guard to let us in.'

After their feast of moistened bread they headed for the river. It was only yards away but it was a struggle with one seriously wounded man leaning heavily on the other whom although not so seriously injured was nevertheless badly wounded.

Cristobal hoisted Sebastian onto his back to ford the river, wading across, carefully seeking out a secure footing with every step. He chuckled wryly, 'No wonder he was made a saint!'

'Who was made a saint?' groaned the passenger.

'My namesake. Of course the water was deeper and the crossing more dangerous and his burden a holy one.'

On the other side they stumbled across another wounded soldier hoping to find sanctuary. His face was a mess of powder burns and congealed blood. He held his hands to his ears, 'Deaf as a post; damned arquebus.'

'A better companion I couldn't have chosen myself. You will be the very help I need and you will have no idea what I or anyone else says about our injured soldier here.'

'Pardon?'

'Precisely, my friend.'

Like three drunken soldiers staggering back to their barracks after a night in the local tavern they finally reached the fort. They stood swaying beneath its walls, calling for admittance.

'Not likely,' was the reply, 'we are overcrowded as it is, and who is to say who you are when it is too dark to tell?'

'Open the gates in the name of King Sebastian.'

'But then you would say that.'

'We are his men, by God's wounds; and honest Portuguese. We must see your captain. It is a question of life or death for a high ranking officer, and of critical importance for our country.'

The dilemma was solved when someone volunteered to come out to identify them as *honest Portuguese.*

Having satisfied the guard they were then permitted to enter, to be escorted directly to the captain's quarters.

Doctors and surgeons attended to the wounds of the man they had been told was the king. Cristobal meanwhile was interrogated by the captain, his two aides, and a priest. He was exhausted, barely able to stand, unable to concentrate on the barrage of hostile questions. He threw up his hands pleading to be allowed to sit, to tell his story in his own words.

The four investigators marvelled at the effrontery of a common soldier daring to ask to be seated in their presence but made this an exception.

He sank onto the wooden stool, closed his eyes for a moment then began. 'Sirs, I can only tell you what I know. It was total chaos. The infidel had us trapped, scything us down at will. Bodies lay in heaps; those still fighting had to scramble over them often only to fall within seconds. Out of the corner of my eye I saw his majesty fending off the enemy with his sword. Then his helmet was sent flying. The next time I saw him he was still brandishing his sword making his way towards the river, stumbling blindly over the fallen. I fought my way towards him flailing at anyone who came near. He was already badly injured, with blood streaming down his face and arm; then he was felled by another blow to the head. I threw myself on top of him.'

Cristobal paused to rest, to gather his thoughts. He used the moment to take the filthy strips of cloth from his forearm to inspect his burning wounds, blowing on them to cool them, gently cupping a protective hand around the gashes. His hands then tentatively explored the bloodied area around his right eye and ear.

'You say the king was on foot. What of his horse?' the priest asked. 'His majesty would never be without his horse.'

'Everyone knows of the king's unrivalled horsemanship,' concurred the captain.

'That's as may be but I said I can only tell you what I know. I never saw a horse. His majesty was on foot with the rest of us. Anyway as soon as he went down I threw myself on top of him. A bit later on I took off all his jewels and somehow or other I pulled off his fancy clothes leaving him in only a chemise and somebody's slop breeches.'

'Impossible, how could you manage such a feat?'

'Please, I beg you to just listen. I have no idea how I managed to do anything except it was a kind of force of will to help my king. Next I pulled dead bodies over us.'

Cristobal knew he had failed to convince them, the story probably did sound far-fetched, but it was true as God was his witness. For a moment he toyed with idea of showing them the jewels but he would need those when they returned to Portugal, and he had every intention of getting his king back to his own land. He waited as they deliberated.

Finally the captain said that while the person in question certainly did resemble the king and they desperately hoped it was his majesty, they would have to wait until the man could speak for himself.

Cristobal didn't know whether to laugh or cry. 'Then we are in a sorry pickle since he says he has no idea who he is, nor what he or any of us are doing here in Morocco.'

'Admiral da Souza will be here soon to take some of the wounded on board. I will have him talk to you since you are the only material witness. Should he decide there is something in what you say you may well soon be on your way to Portugal. Have the doctor see to your wounds.'

As Cristobal left the room the captain called to him, 'I pray to God that this man is, as you insist, King Sebastian, or that the people of Portugal believe him to be so, otherwise our country is in serious danger of being ruled by King Philip and his Spaniards.'

'And that's another problem,' Cristobal replied. 'He says that if he is the king he is too ashamed to let people know right now, says if he is he has to do twenty years penance, get absolution from the Pope.'

Chapter 8

To anyone looking in at Ana's small private chapel it would have appeared that she and her two friends were on their knees in prayer, whereas they were far too busy talking as they knelt before the altar.

'Do you truly believe our two years of prayers and the candles are doing any good?'

'Why ever not?' answered Louisa. 'Sister Isabel says that King Sebastian is still alive so our prayers will make it doubly positive that he is.'

'And,' insisted Maria, 'you must remember that King Philip has not lost the war in the Low Countries. Although the commander has died; a new commander has taken over and he is just as victorious they say. So, there you are, the candles work. In any case we have been doing it so long it would be silly to stop now, even should Sister Isabel allow it.'

'And she certainly would not,' commented Isabel peeping in at the chapel door.

So many extra prayers had been said for the soul of His Excellency Don Juan of Austria who had died fighting for his king. Many of their prayers had been said in the main chapel with all those miserable nuns. Ana hated that chapel, hated the oppressive congregation of black habited old women chanting the same old prayers day in day out. She used those Masses to think of Lady Aunt Magdalena and how sad she must be feeling; while very little affection was ever shown towards her there had always been plenty to shower on Juan.

Ana got up from her knees, 'I think we have done enough praying today and we should go into the orchard to play. Sister Isabel, may we?'

'Of course, you have done all your studies and duties. I shall come for you when it is time for dinner. Run along, but make sure you dress well against the cold.'

Cloaks were snatched and thrown about their shoulders as they raced to be first to the door, only to run straight into Sister Leonor, the *key lady*.

'Such behaviour; Sister Isabel your discipline continues to leave a lot to be desired.'

'Sorry, Sister Leonor,' the girls chanted, 'may we go now?'

'Certainly not; a letter has arrived for you, an important letter.'

A letter; it was a letter; a letter for her; an important letter for her. Ana had not received a letter in the four or more years she had lived here. She reached to take it from the reluctant looking messenger.

Sister Leonor gave every indication of not wishing to part with it, her claws keeping it tight against her bony chest.

'Please may I have my letter?' Ana moved closer to take it. The precious piece of paper was now in her hands. She treasured this moment; she was holding *her* letter, turning it, examining the imprint on the seal.

'Are you not going to open it?' Sister Leonor snapped.

'Not yet.' This may be the only letter she would ever receive so she determined to make the most of it, and she certainly did not want Sister Leonor to be present when she finally did open it. No, she would definitely wait.

When it became obvious that the letter was not about to be opened Sister Leonor left to return to the prioress to say that she had carried out her instructions.

Ana turned the letter once more until it was the right way up. There was a line of the neatest and most perfectly formed writing stating *Her Excellency Doña Ana de Austria*. She read it and re-read it, trying to believe.

Carefully, so as not to beak the beautiful red wax seal, Ana pushed her finger underneath until seal and paper were separated and the letter could be unfolded.

She read the contents aloud, '*Serene Princess, Doña Ana de Austria, It is with the heaviest of hearts that I have to write of the death of your father. I was at the side of His Excellency Don Juan when he departed this life for a much better world.* Sister Isabel I am a princess and Don Juan was my father; can you believe it? What does it say next? *The last two years were most difficult for him but he faced them with courage and fortitude, the like I have never known or shall ever know again. I shall miss him sorely; we had been friends for many a year and I loved* him as I would the dearest of brothers. I am sure you will have heard all the accolades regarding his leadership against the Moors, the Turk, and the rebels of the Low Countries, and I shall not repeat them here except to say that the blood of his father, Emperor Charles V certainly coursed through his veins. Instead I wish to say something about the man who was your father.'

Ana could not see to read any more her eyes brimmed with tears, 'I have to keep saying it, Don Juan was my father, I had a father all along, but I was never allowed to know. Read it for me, Sister Isabel.' She cried into her handkerchief.

'Gladly, my dear. *This is to say something about the man who was your father. Try not to think too ill of Don Juan. It was his destiny to serve his king and country, to be a great leader and not a father. I do know that he loved your mother dearly and had circumstances been different they would have married and you and your brother would have been part of a very happy family. But those of the nobility cannot choose the life they might most desire.*

I searched for some remembrance for you but he died a poor man the army expenses digging deep into his purse forcing him to sell everything of value. What I can send are his words of love for you his Little Abbess and his sorrow that he had never been a father to you and given you a home.

I have assumed the duties of commander and pray to God I might be as good a leader as Don

Juan and bring these wars to a quick end to honour his name.

With great affection, I kiss your hand dear cousin,

Alessandro, Duque di Parma.'

Ana dried her eyes and took the letter to read it again and again.

Sister Isabel looked at this child who over the years had become almost her daughter and who was, in fact, Her Excellency Doña Ana de Austria, King Philip's niece.

Ana was not the first royal child to be shut away in this monastery; two kings to Isabel's certain knowledge had had their illegitimate daughters hidden away behind these walls. It was interesting to discover Ana's true identity; it now explained why the king's lawyer had been a signatory along with Doña Magdalena committing the child to this particular Augustinian order.

Louisa broke the silence. 'Will you be leaving the monastery?'

'I must. I want to be free of this hateful place. But you will all come with me; I could never leave you behind.'

Sister Isabel drew Ana to her side, 'Dear child, do not set your hopes too high, remember it was the will of his majesty as well as your aunt that you become a novitiate.'

'But all that has changed now. I shall write to the king to explain I have no wish to become a nun, never will have. If he could make my father, his half-brother, into a commander he can surely make me into a lady-in-waiting or something like that. He could definitely find a place for me somewhere.'

'And in the meantime you could ask the king to tell you who is your mother,' Maria was as excited as Ana.

'Girls,' Sister Isabel cautioned, 'let us enjoy this moment of discovery. Ana, you have spent years as an orphan with no other name than Ana. Now, like Louisa and Maria, you have a family. Let us rejoice in that and give our thanks to God. I think we should go to the chapel.'

The friends filed obediently past Isabel: Louisa and Maria basking in the fortune of their friend and imagining exciting possibilities for themselves; Ana's thoughts were here, there, and everywhere. She was a princess, Don Juan was her father, and it was her father who had given her the beloved doll. She had a mother who had been loved by her father. She had a brother somewhere who must be a prince; her cousins were the Princesses Isabel Clara Eugenia and Catalina Micaela. The Duque di Parma was her cousin; her grandfather had been an emperor as well as the king of Spain. She was going to leave this place to meet some of her family. She would marry and live happily ever after with a husband and a family; her dreams and fantasies becoming a reality.

They passed gossiping groups of nuns. Some stopped to smile and greet her whispering, 'Your Excellency'; others decided to ignore the young princess.

The news was out, no doubt spread by Sister Leonor, and the convent was apparently already divided into two distinct camps.

Chapter 9

As the day progressed so the rain fell heavier than ever and by late afternoon the two riders were seeking refuge deep inside their waterproof cloaks, wide brimmed hats pulled tight down about their ears. They leaned along their horses' necks hoping for further protection.

One of the men raised his head shouting out against the racket of thundering horse hooves, groaning leather and jangling harness. Stung and choked by the lashing torrent he called, 'Are we still headed in the right direction do you suppose, Cristobal?'

'I pray so my lord; that is definitely a monastery up ahead.'

'Thank God for that. We need to get out of these wet things and next to a welcoming fire.' He laughed, 'We were told that northwest Spain can be very wet; I never understood until now what they meant by wet.'

At last they were at the monastery gates and Cristobal pulled on the bell rope. Someone must have been keeping watch, awaiting their arrival, because without any delay the heavy wooden doors swung open.

A flurry of black robed monks helped them dismount, two took charge of their travel satchels; two led the horses away as another two escorted them to the prior's apartments.

The prior, small, rotund and jolly looking had come out into the chill of the cloister to welcome them.

'Welcome sirs,' he beamed at them opening his arms wide as if to gather them in from the storm. 'Not the best of days to be abroad; Brother Miguel show these gentlemen to their room, see to it they have dry, warm robes, then bring them back to me. Sirs, I await your return with great impatience.' He watched them for a while before disappearing into the enveloping warmth of his chambers, glad to shut the door on so miserable a day.

A diminutive Brother Miguel conducted the travellers through the cloister ushering them through a door and along a cold stone corridor and into a room that had obviously been prepared for them. It was comfortable enough; there were two beds, a table, a couple of chairs and a fireplace of crackling logs and cheery flames.

Black woollen habits lay in readiness on the beds and they quickly stripped off wet boots, dripping jerkins, breeches, chemises. They threw the robes of accommodating one-size-fits-all over their heads and adjusted and fastened them tight at their waist with a length of cord. Sandals were strapped on and they were ready.

'Dry clothes; I think I never knew such joy, Cristobal. What do you think; do we pass as lay brothers?'

As they were changing Brother Miguel shook out their wet belongings arranging them over the chairs to merrily steam before the fire. All the while he was studying the two guests.

One was slightly taller than average, had blue eyes and blond hair. For certain there was a hint of lameness about one of the legs, cleverly disguised perhaps by years of determined exercise. There was a scar on his left temple and hairline, and there were the remains of some ugly injuries down his right arm and, dear Lord, yes, a finger was missing. He crossed himself at the necessary evil of wars. The other man, he noted, was not quite so tall but still of a goodly height and was uncannily like his companion, even to the extent of having wounds about his temple and ear. The poor fellow's back was a veritable network of healed wounds.

'*Bem vinido a sua majestade. Eu sou seu servo e servirá como Deuns commandos. Espero que Portugal terá em breve o seu legitimo monarco*'.

The two riders started, exchanging worried glances.

'Sorry, what was that?' It was Cristobal who spoke, 'We couldn't understand a word.'

'I beg your pardon gentlemen I mistakenly thought you to be Portuguese.' He reddened; embarrassed and flustered.

'No problem; sorry to disappoint you, we are nothing other than Spanish. Shall we go to the prior?'

Brother Miguel hurried them back through the cloisters to the prior's rooms continuing his muttered apologies.

The prior set his quill aside, wiped his ink stained fingers on a much-used piece of blackened rag, and rose to greet them.

'Come in, come in. Do have some mulled wine, excellent for warming the body and spirit. I am proud to say that this wine was selected from our very best; the deepest red and full of body for a young wine. It has been flavoured with melon and a little cinnamon and heated to just the right temperature.'

Three silver goblets were raised in a toast. 'Good health, your grace, and our deepest gratitude for your hospitality.'

'Your majesty, I am more than delighted to help in any way. When I received the letter from Doña Tabora requesting we make you welcome here for as long as you wish to remain, I can tell you I leapt at the opportunity.'

'Please call me Gabriel. We still have no idea who I am, so I have taken on the name Gabriel de Espinosa. It will serve me well enough until hopefully my memory is restored.'

Cristobal protested, 'You say *we* have no idea; *you* may have no idea but I know exactly who you are!'

It was the prior's turn to protest, 'Since you know this is His Majesty King Sebastian it behoves you to show more respect.'

'And no disrespect meant, your grace; it's a part of our strategy.'

Gabriel nodded. 'That is true, we travel as two friends. Prior, you mentioned Doña Tabora, a most saintly woman and I ask you to remember her in your prayers. She spared neither effort nor expense to see we had the best of physicians to return us to health. And remember Cristobal here, too, for were it not for him there would have been no need for any doctors.'

The prior raised his goblet, 'Portugal will be forever grateful, Don Cristobal.'

'I was and always will be only too ready to lay down my life for my master. But Portugal must not set her hopes too high for the king's return.'

'Not return to Portugal, when everyone is desperate for the *Desired One*? May I ask what it is you propose to do instead?'

'Father, if I am indeed the king then I have brought dishonour on myself and shame on my people thrusting them under the heel of the enemy. In my estimation it will take twenty years of penance to scourge my soul of the cankerworm of pride and arrogance that has dragged them down into this mire. What I hope to do is to work for my daily bread, seek out wrongs and put them to rights, make my way to Rome to throw myself on the mercy of the Pope then travel to Jerusalem. Once I am absolved I hope to retire with my friend into obscurity far from this peninsular; in Naples or Sicily, who knows? In the long run there should be no fears for Portugal, I certainly have none. I honestly believe that eventually a monarch will emerge from the Royal House of Braganza, someone far worthier than I could ever be, and Spain will never dare violate her borders again. Well; that must be the longest speech I ever made.'

'I have to admit to being bitterly disappointed, but I respect your decision. Be that as it may, you have set yourself an onerous task. You have decided on a long and arduous journey, physically and spiritually; how can I help?'

'To begin with, your grace, by allowing us to work for a while in your stables.'

A broad smile puffed out the prior's ruby cheeks. 'I have heard of King Sebastian's equestrian fame, but mastering horses is a far cry from stable lads' work. I think that for hands as fine as yours, and one can see that they are indeed fine, some work as a *pastelero,* a pastry chef, would be more suitable. One of my, our, weaknesses is fine pastries; no dessert is complete without them. Would that be an acceptable challenge for you?'

'I am at your command; if you wish me to be a *pastelero* then that is what I shall be; and Cristobal too.'

The prior nodded his assent. 'So that is done. Do sit down. Have some more wine, and I insist you sample our pilgrims' biscuits; a little drop of liqueur in the mixture lends a most satisfying flavour.' His smile was a bit shamefaced,

'Goodness me you must think we are constantly indulging ourselves; and you might just be right!'

Gabriel and Cristobal munched on the tiny biscuits with their little hole at the centre. They closed their eyes the better to savour the aniseed.

'Caution is called for, Cristobal, or we could get used to this life.'

The prior became serious, 'Over the next few months I would like you to do me the favour of considering a proposal.' He lowered his voice, 'I know of a young gentleman, no more than a boy really, living with his uncle. He is of a noble line and is in need of a tutor.'

'It should be easy enough to find one; many would be eager enough for such a position.'

'Quite so, but it would suit me if you were to be that tutor.'

'That would encourage people to ask questions about my background.'

Cristobal scratched at his forehead, 'How right you are Gabriel, and that would be a bit of a worry; which reminds me about that monk Miguel. What was he after, talking to us in Portuguese? What does he know?'

'You worry too much, young man. Brother Miguel has been exiled from Portugal because of past political involvement, but although unable to live in his beloved country he continues with his unfulfilled wish for the Portuguese Prior of Crato, Don Antonio, to become Portugal's monarch. Because of this he is in constant touch with Brethren in Portugal and France, desperate for any snippet of information however true or false. Rest assured there is nothing more to the man than that. As to my suggestion of your becoming a tutor you will find no problems there either. How shall I put it? You, Gabriel, and this gentleman of the Mendoza family would both be making me, an old man, very happy. I want to help you both, do you see? You are both on a mission of sorts. You, Gabriel, following the disastrous Battle of Alcazarquivir, are determined on your long pilgrimage towards absolution, either for yourself or King Sebastian. The Mendoza gentleman wishes to ensure a nobleman's education for his nephew, an orphaned boy, the son of Don Juan of Austria.'

Cristobal explained, 'Gabriel, seeing as how you seem not to remember anything before the battle, you won't recall the gossip, sir, that Don Juan was never allowed to marry but he did have quite an affair going with a beautiful young lady. Lasted ages it did, pretty heated too by all accounts.'

The prior tut-tutted, 'Quite so, young man. As you say the relationship lasted for some years. His Majesty King Philip had Don Juan sent abroad to command the army and the navy and that put an end to any romance. Sadly the fruit of this relationship has been denied his parenthood and his rights. The least we can do is to give this boy the education a nobleman requires before setting out into the world to seek his fortune. At the same time I earnestly wish to give you, too, the means by which to survive.'

'Gabriel, there was more to that Don Juan business than that. There is a girl somewhere, a daughter. Am I right; Father?'

The prior nodded, 'Her Excellency Doña Ana of Austria.'

'What fortune for the girl, Father; she, at least was recognised!'

'Not a bit of it; she is hidden away in a convent, it being the king's will that she remain there for the rest of her days. There is nothing we can do for her but we can help the boy.'

'And I am the right person?'

'Of course; you are an educated man, whoever you are Gabriel, with a memory for everything except your past. You have the greatest skills in horsemanship, fencing, and swimming; your ability for foreign languages is second to none. You cannot tell me I have been misled with this information, Doña Tabora and many others who have met you cannot all be wrong.'

Gabriel laughed, 'It seems you know more about me than I know myself. I shall consider your offer.'

Chapter 10

Ana was now seventeen years old; her two friends had taken the veil while she doggedly continued in her refusal. Her nun's *habit* was of the finest black silk and she wore her white wimple pushed back on her head to reveal her blond curls which she vowed would never be cut off. She had also begun to wear jewellery; just a touch here and there, a brooch or two, a necklace, and rings.

She had endured years of frustrated letter writing to her Lady Aunt Magdalena and to her uncle, the king, without ever receiving one word of reply. She had screamed and raged against her imprisonment, and as a consequence had been subjected to enforced blood lettings to rid her of whatever was having such an evil influence over her. She had been ill often enough to weaken her delicate frame but definitely not her determination to never, ever, becoming a nun.

It was a pale and red eyed Ana who stood at the table with her friends Louisa, Maria, and Isabel on this early afternoon in September.

An unopened letter from Lady Aunt Magdalena lay on the table. It had been delivered by Sister Leonor, the *key lady*, shortly after the special mass at which the aunt had offered candles and a further five hundred *ducados* for Ana to take the veil. The aunt had left immediately afterwards without a word.

'Having said nothing for years and not deigning to visit me, what can there possibly be of interest in this?' Ana flicked the piece of paper across the table. 'Not even sealed, no doubt a few eyes have already studies its contents.'

'All the same, Ana, please open it, we are curious.' Louisa pushed the letter back to her.

She unfolded it and scanned a few lines, 'This is a lecture, reminding me, lest I should have forgotten, that there are two alternatives for ladies such as us; marriage or seclusion. Marriage has been denied me, therefore only the cloister remains.' She crumpled the hateful piece of paper in her hand, screaming between clenched teeth, 'I refuse to be a nun!'

Louisa commiserated, 'How many of us are in this convent for that very same reason. How many of us would prefer a different life to this?'

'But Louisa I thought that being a princess and with my money all that would change.'

Maria saw no point to their going over the same old ground yet again, 'What else does she have to say?'

'She refuses to reveal the names of any of my family. Hopefully, Louisa, your brother can do that for me. She says it would be the ruination of their lives!' Ana got up and stormed about the room.

Isabel hurried to her side, 'Doña Magdalena has a point. The king has commanded you to take the veil. How would it look if you were to approach anyone to support your cause? Well let me tell you, it will bring great displeasure to his majesty; by that I mean anyone offering their help would be constituting dissent punishable by at the very best the loss of their royal incomes and their status. You should also consider your own position; you might find yourself no longer a princess, no longer in receipt of your royal income. All things are his majesty's to give or take away.'

'Why has life been so unkind to me? Why was I not allowed to know my father, hidden away in this place; and why, when I was offered the chance to marry, live in Italy, have a family of my own, why was it snatched away?'

Maria shrugged, 'Probably because the suitor is related to the Pope and Philip finds the papal nuncio intolerable.'

Isabel poured drinks of refreshing lemon and invited Ana back to the table. 'The sad fact is that you are too important a princess. Think of it: niece of the king, cousin of Alessandro Farnese and King Sebastian – if he still lives. If you were to marry you would be handing your spouse a lot of power.' She urged them to huddle closer, whispering, 'King Philip's daughter, Princess Isabel Clara Eugenia is in exactly the same position. Yes, she does live in a palace surrounded by courtiers and no doubt suitors, but for all the luxuries of the royal court she can only wander its salons and corridors in isolated splendour. It could well be that she may never have a husband for the very same reasons that apply to you. To mention but two: she is older and far more intelligent than her young half-brother who is heir; he is male and she is female and there lie the differences.'

There was a knock on the door and Sister Leonor entered, sneering, 'My word but you look like conspirators. Don Blas has arrived and is waiting in the *locutorio*.'

'Good, then we must go immediately,' Ana pushed the letter deep inside a pocket in her robe. She called to her servant Dorotea, 'Take some drinks to the *locutorio* as quickly as you can. Oh, friends, fingers crossed that everything has worked out well!'

Blas Nieto paced about the *locutorio* on the far side of the lattice stopping to cross himself each time he passed beneath the painting of Saint Augustine. As soon as he heard the door opening he strode over to greet them, 'I thought you would never come, I have been here quite some time.'

'Forgive us Don Blas, we have only just been informed.'

'How are you, brother, and is our family well?'

'Most well, but of that later; I have much more important items of interest to talk about, and who knows if that dreaded *key lady* might take it upon herself to intrude.'

'She will be sent away. Do be seated, Don Blas. Ah, Dorotea, offer Don Blas some wine.'

Louisa, Maria, and Isabel were only slightly surprised that Blas had been invited to sit in the princess's company, only visitors of the same social standing should be allowed to sit; but then Ana was anything but conventional.

Blas unbuckled his sword and laid it with his hat, cloak, and satchel on the long bench by the wall. He removed a sheaf of papers from his satchel and placed them by the jar of wine on the table before settling himself into his chair.

'Your Excellency, I expect you to be nothing less than delighted with my endeavours. Without further delay then; your mother was Maria Mendoza, a member of that renowned and noble family.'

'Was?'

'Yes, alas she died shortly after your father, many say of a broken heart. Theirs was a very passionate affair I understand; at one time she even dressed as a man to follow him secretly to Granada. It was there that a boy was born.'

'It is true, I have a brother!'

'Francisco was abducted by the Moors, later to be ransomed by the family. It is all written down here.'

'Will he visit?'

'So far as I know he is unaware of your existence. But if I may press on, I would hate to be interrupted, you also have a sister Juana, in Italy. She was being cared for by your Aunt Marguerita di Parma until the king commanded she enter a convent. Again I have made several notes for you on this.'

He stopped to allow himself a sip of wine.

'Your Excellency you may find the next part distressing and I do not wish to offend.'

'Do go on, dear friend,'

'Prince Michele has married into the Mendoza family.'

Ana Swallowed hard; so, her suitor had married. In truth her own marriage to him had probably all been the vainest of hopes, a young girl's romantic dream. There had been some wonderful days reading tender letters of love, of receiving beautiful gifts – she looked at her diamond brooches in their engraved silver settings – but that was all in the past, her longed-for husband was wed to another.

Blas cleared his throat in apology, 'I shall pass on to something else. Your German grandmother is living in Spain, in Santander. A fiery woman if ever there was one, and something of an embarrassment to the king. He insisted she retire to a convent, but she would have none of it. And she succeeded!'

All four ladies gasped their astonishment at the defiance.

'And she told Doña Magdalena de Ulloa never to mention it again. Perhaps the king conceded defeat suspecting that she would have had a most unsettling affect on a community of innocent nuns.'

Ana clapped her hands, 'But how exquisitely bold of her!'

'The king demands she is known as Madame Blomberg and not the Emperor Charles V's widow.'

Ana was delighted, 'She is indeed a very bold lady, I must write to her.'

'Once again Your Excellency,' he tapped his sheaf of papers, 'there is much more to read in here.'

'You have given me much to think on. Blas, you are quite a wonder. Anything more, or am I being greedy?'

'The Princess of Eboli, your mother's relative, yet another bold lady has been imprisoned. At one time she was the king's mistress before switching her attentions to his secretary. Apparently she has used her wiles to discover the code used in letters to and from Portugal. I give more information in here. Which brings me neatly to the Portuguese problem; do come closer.

The chairs were pulled close to the lattice.

Blas continued, 'A former preacher in the Royal House of Avis was, after the assumed death of King Sebastian, actively supporting the claims of Don Antonio, the Prior of Crato. To cut a long story short he was captured and brought to Spain to be kept under close observation. He is in a monastery at Salamanca but is soon to be sent here by order of King Philip to be the new vicar of this convent.'

'Of all the convents in Spain, why here?' Ana looked from one to the other of her companions.

'It sounds highly suspicious to me,' Maria offered.

Isabel would have none of it, 'You are allowing your imaginations to run wild. This is a royal monastery with very close connections to the reigning monarch; there could not be a more suitable place for his majesty to lodge someone who at one time was found to be an enemy and who is now reformed. He can never have posed any danger or he would have been disposed of long ago; is that not so, Don Bas?'

'Precisely, Sister Isabel.'

'I doubt I shall sleep tonight, there is so much to think about.' Ana passed a small package containing two pairs of fine leather gloves through the lattice, 'Please accept this gift as a small token of my appreciation of all your efforts. I shall now leave you and your sisters to enjoy a private family visit.'

The bulky sheaf of delicious information was handed to Ana and she left the *locutorio* clutching it to her breast.

Chapter 11

Ana stormed along the arcade of the cloister headed for the *locutorio*, the hem of her black woollen habit kicked up by angry heels. For the first time in months her pallid face with its lifeless eyes was animated with the heightened colour of indignation. She stopped.

'Father Miguel, whatever makes the lady presume I would wish to meet her?'

Father Miguel, the vicar of the convent for the last eight years, was scurrying along behind her immersed in his own thoughts and almost collided with her, 'Perhaps, my lady, some message from Doña Magdalena?'

His Portuguese accent had lost nothing of its strangeness to her ears. He spoke with the same speed as his hurried movements, the words clipped short and accompanied often with a whistle of sorts.

'Hardly likely! Years ago I worshipped this lady, this Condessa de Salinas. She was everything an impressionable child would want to be when she grew up: beautiful, rich, happy, carefree. And she turned out to be the shallowest, most thoughtless, and proudest of creatures. She has probably come to gloat; the family have got their way at last.'

'I have told you several times that all is not lost by your taking the veil; remember the story of

Don Antonio, the Prior of Crato, and his uncompleted vows.'

'I know, I know. As for the condessa you shall soon see that I am correct in every way.' Ana pushed her wimple back on her head defiantly revealing some of her golden curls; she may have become a nun but not one hair on her head had been ravaged by those who had been eagerly waiting with the scissors.

'You are not averse to a little pride yourself, my lady.'

'And why not? I have precious little else! Oh, the sooner this is over the better.'

She strode into the room and across to the grille where she stood seething.

The condessa smiled, 'Sister Ana, how good it is to see you.'

'Good to see me as a nun, you mean. Finally your cares are over.'

'That is most unkind. I came to offer you my congratulations and best wishes.'

'Condessa, I have been imprisoned in this place for fourteen years, since I was but an infant of six years. You must remember as it was you who brought me here. Throughout those long years of suffering, and you know full well how I have suffered, you visited on one occasion only – to bring votive candles for King Sebastian, who I pray to God is still alive, and for my father, Don Juan de Austria, God rest his soul.'

'I was unable to ...'

'It seems I must formally announce that the Ana who had been ailing and suffering for fourteen years is now quite dead to the world and therefore no longer requires visitors. Did you bring the candles for the prayers for the dead?'

'Ana, I am shocked; I never expected this. I will not tolerate your rudeness,' she put her handkerchief to her lips.

'Alas, one can never prepare oneself for the unexpected, condessa.'

The condessa rose to go then just as quickly sat down again. 'I find myself facing a dilemma. I cannot leave at this moment; there is a disturbance in the square.'

For an instant Ana thought that one of her fairy tale dreams might have become a reality. She clutched at her doll tucked in the pocket of her robes then chided herself at her stupidity.

The condessa continued, 'Apparently there is a stallion gone wild or crazy and no one seems capable of quieting it. It would be far too dangerous for me to set foot outside. I only pray my horses and carriage are safe.'

'And any unfortunate villagers who may find themselves innocent victims! If you do intend staying here for a while I suggest you either visit the prioress or send for Sister Leonor; both excellent company I am sure. And, by the by, condessa, as Her Excellency Doña Ana de Austria, I do give you my permission to sit. Perhaps your manners as well as court etiquette were left in the carriage, or you felt you had no need of them here. Father Miguel, would you accompany me to my apartments?' She allowed herself a congratulatory smile.

'My lady that was most uncharitable of you,' Father Miguel admonished, pulling himself up to his full height leaving him still several inches shorter than Ana.

'Not a bit of it, it was fun. After fourteen years I have had my say; small consolation for a reluctant nun, compelled against her will ...'

'As I repeatedly remind you, Don Antonio the Prior of Crato and rightful heir to the throne of Portugal, never ...'

'Heir to the throne only if King Sebastian is dead, may I remind you!'

'If King Sebastian is dead,' the vicar conceded. 'But to continue, Don Antonio had never wanted to be a priest, and eventually wrote to tell the Pope of his circumstances. He was released from all his vows. In your case your enforced novitiate is contrary to the ruling of the Council of Trent and your vows are therefore null and void. All you need is patience.' He looked about them to make sure they were alone to whisper. 'Yes, patience; for as soon as King Philip is dead I have a letter already prepared for immediate despatch to His Holiness. Believe, have faith.'

Ana took his hands in hers, 'You are right, I do at least have that one dream to cling to. Now I must be out of these appalling robes. My satins with a few jewels will lift my spirits. And later we will celebrate today in our own special way; cook has been busy since early morning. A banquet is called for, to be shared with friends.'

'I have been impatient all day to tell you of something equally special. At times it has been almost impossible to contain myself; I have longed to tell you that a gift has arrived. It came by carriage, and I have had to find various ways to keep it concealed from you. Now is the moment for you to see it.'

'A gift, for me; where is it?'

'It is now in your apartments, under the watchful eye of your manservant Roderos.'

'Good Lord, but we must hurry.'

Ana burst into the salon to find Roderos standing guard over a dirty and very battered wicker travelling basket.

Disappointment flooded over Ana, yet what had she expected, an unknown family visitor, a fairy tale prince? When would she ever grow up? Father Miguel had never referred to the gift as anything other than *it*; she told herself again that she really must try harder to rid herself of childish dreams even if they had been her strength for years.

The vicar smiled with a sympathy reserved for an unhappy child, 'Trust me, my lady. Roderos quickly now, open the basket.'

A peg was pulled free and the lid lifted, the young lad reached inside and brought out a handful of shivering curly dark wool. The wriggling creature was lowered to the floor, and Ana sank to her knees beside it. She gazed incredulous at this ball of curls all black except for a white muzzle.

The puppy hesitated then skittered off here, there, and everywhere, tiny claws slipping and sliding over the tiles, sending it crashing into table legs, disappearing under chests. After several failed attempts it jumped up on the dais to scramble amongst the cushions. Then it was down again to skate across the floor to investigate Roderos' shoes and Father Miguel's rosary before finding Ana's lap.

She cradled it in her hands holding it close to her face, rewarded by a series of wet licks from the tiniest of pink tongues. 'You little darling,' she cried, 'Dorotea, a bowl of water is needed here, quickly. What sort of dog is it, does anyone know?'

The vicar knew, 'A type of Portuguese Water Dog, but a very small version, a lap dog.'

'Portuguese; how strange; did you have anything to do with this? Who sent it, where from, is there a note?'

A bowl was set down and the puppy lapped noisily, oblivious to his enraptured audience.

'So, what do we know of the puppy?'

'Nothing, my lady, except that the coachman said I was to tell you that it was a gift from a Don Francisco.'

'Then it must be from my brother! Somehow or other my brother knows I am here! But there must be a note.'

Roderos rummaged among the cloths at the bottom of the basket until finally, 'Yes, here is something.'

Ana tore it open, to be disappointed once more, it was nothing but the simplest of notes *I am thinking of you* and written in a poor quality ink, barely legible.

Father Miguel pursed his lips, tapped the tip of his nose with his forefinger, 'Of course; if you will allow me, I shall take the note.' And off he went.

Ana sent for Isabel and friends Louisa and Maria to come and join in the fun. As they played with the puppy they tried to choose a name for it but became so busy enjoying its antics that Father Miguel had returned before any decision could be made.

The note was handed to Ana, and Father Miguel stood to one side wearing the broadest of grins.

Ana read, '*I hope this lap dog will bring you many years of happiness. I would so dearly have loved to have brought her myself but in these days of distrust and suspected treason, no matter how groundless, it is out of the question. Dearest sister you are often in my thoughts, I kiss your hands with brotherly affection. Don Francisco.*'

'You see; my brother does know I am here! He has written me a letter. I shall cherish this always. What is wrong with the world, demanding such secrecy, denying families being together?'

'My lady, we do not want to cloud such a happy occasion with any dark thoughts. Suffice it to say your brother is being sensible in not advertising that he knows where you are or revealing his own whereabouts. These are difficult days when the king is suspicious of everyone and everything; but we will say no more on the matter.'

'As usual you are so right. Tell me instead of this mysterious letter and what you had to do to retrieve it.'

'Oh, that is of no importance, just something I remembered having witnessed long ago.'

'But you made the short note disappear and now we have this letter.'

'I assure you there was nothing to it. I got some oak galls from the convent pharmacy, made a mixture, brushed it over the paper, and the rest you know. I surprised myself remembering the method; but there you are, simply good fortune in remembering.'

Ana laughed, 'And at the same time you have solved a problem for me. I shall call the puppy Fortuna.'

Chapter 12

'My lady, this is the person I said would make a welcome addition to your staff, someone noted for the excellence of his sweet pastries and desserts. This is Señor Gabriel de Espinosa; *pastelero.*

Ana motioned to Louisa and Maria to sit, Father Miguel placed her chair close to the grille and she sat down ensuring Fortuna was comfortable in her lap. She leaned forward towards the visitor until her eyes became accustomed to the gloom.

She was puzzled by what she saw; because what she saw certainly did not look like anything she expected. All the other men of her acquaintance were priests and wore robes so she only had her manservant Roderos to compare him with. This person was much, much older and looked stronger, but more than this, his bearing was quite – dare she say it – noble. Awakening memories of Villagarcía and her father, the handsome Don Juan de Austria, further convinced her; she was right, this was no servant, no tradesman, this was a gentleman.

Leaning back in her chair and resting her chin on her hands she spent some time studying this pastry cook. Everything about this person spoke of refinement: his brown doublet and hose, admittedly not of the best of materials, was well cut; the show of fine holland at his neck and wrists; the bonnet in his hands with its small jewelled brooch, nothing ostentatious but they were still jewels. He held his head high, and it was a well-favoured head with blond hair and trimmed beard. He was fair skinned with pale blue eyes. Was her imagination playing wilful tricks on her or did he actually remind her of her father? She had also noticed the scars about his temple speaking of gallantry in battle; the inevitable wounds. The longer she studied him the more she was convinced he was someone of rank.

She beckoned Father Miguel, 'I have very little experience of this world, but I am no dolt. This is no *pastelero*.'

'In a sense you are correct, my lady. If you will be patient everything can be explained.'

'Well, I have always enjoyed a good story; Heaven knows that is how I have filled so many lonely days and nights, this is how I have survived in this dreadful place, so I am eager to hear yours.'

'It begins with the disturbance in the square a few weeks ago; the incident of the runaway horse.'

'Ah, the day the condessa said she would not dare leave the safety of the convent.' Ana remembered the interview well.

'The very one; there was no one able or courageous enough to assist the terrified rider until Señor Gabriel de Espinosa here and his friend rode into the square,' he invited Gabriel to speak, 'Do you wish to continue the tale, señor?'

'Your Excellency, Doña Ana, there is little to tell.'

It was almost impossible for Ana to follow his tale; his voice was absolute enchantment, creating within her the strangest of sensations. It was a voice of exquisite resonance, a dark and mellow voice with a hint of an accent that thrilled.

The voice continued, 'What I did was nothing extraordinary. I have always enjoyed working with horses; they are so intelligent, bold, strong, the most beautiful of creatures. I did no more than dismount and approach the unfortunate animal. You must understand that the stallion was distraught and this was the reason for its behaviour. I vaulted on to its back, reached round the rider to take the reins and within minutes the poor beast was calm. Apparently the rider, a young lad and no horseman, had been too demanding without the expertise to execute those very demands.'

Ana was drowning in images of this robust and quite handsome man with the voice that thrilled executing such daring deeds. Here was one of the princes of her fairy tales.

Father Miguel's eyes twinkled with mischief, 'Except that by the time the full story reached my ears it had the added fact that the hero of the day was also a *pastelero*. It took little effort on my part to realise that here was something that had to be more than a coincidence.'

'And what coincidence would that be?'

'That I could have come across another man adept with horses and pastry.'

Ana replied, 'Whereas I find it quite incredible that there could be even one pastry chef and an expert equestrian all in one.'

She warned herself to be careful; a dolt she may not be, but vulnerable she certainly was. Father Miguel could be gullible too, always seeing the best in everyone, and he was asking her to consider taking this person into her household. She changed the position of her chair that she could keep both the vicar and the *pastelero* in view.

The vicar continued, 'My lady, as you know many years ago I was brought to this country to be kept under observation because of my support for Don Antonio, Prior of Crato, and of the Portuguese Royal House of Braganza, in his attempted accession to the throne of Portugal. It was while I was being held in the monastery near Salamanca that I met a lay priest, a fine horseman who wished to become a pastry chef. Apparently it was some kind of penance. Recently, when I heard of the events in the square and that the hero of the day was also the new owner of the pastry shop I had to visit to see for myself. And there he was, with his friend Cristobal, just as in those bygone days. His pastries are delicious and you deserve better than your cook's feeble offerings.'

'Father Miguel, I can understand you wishing me to grant an audience to the fearless man who can dominate horses, and I appreciate your excitement on meeting an old acquaintance; but they seem scant reasons for me to employ him as my pastry chef, however much you think I need one.'

There was a very long and awkward silence. Ana looked from the vicar to the *pastelero*. For her the strangest coincidence by far was the fact that the two men should now find themselves in this fairly remote little town. Yet she had no cause to doubt the vicar. Although she knew virtually nothing of Father Miguel's history prior to his appointment to this convent – and that would certainly account for his never speaking of a horseman-cum-pastry cook – he had been vicar now for some years and was thoroughly dependable.

As for this Gabriel fellow; those blue eyes, the windows to his soul, they positively shone integrity; and that wonderful voice surely made his honesty unquestionable. And yet she still doubted. There had to be something more; something was being withheld.

It was the *pastelero* who eventually spoke, 'Father Miguel, one of us must proceed or all will be lost, you have done nothing but raise unnecessary suspicions. My lady, when the vicar visited my shop it was the ideal opportunity for me to ask him if you had received the puppy. This, after all, is the true reason for my presence in Madrigal and in this convent today.'

Ana stroked her little *baby*, picked her up to plant kisses on her ears, 'How could you possibly know about my darling Fortuna?' This was bewildering.

'I was with your brother when he decided to send it, and I assisted with the secret message.' Gabriel laughed, 'I had heard that Father Miguel was here and therefore I knew he would be aware that concealed in the note there was an intended greeting. He has had years of practice, keeping in touch with Don Antonio and his supporters in France and Portugal as well as in Spain. Is that not true Father Miguel?' He laughed again, his laughter flooding the room with its vitality and bringing echoes of a complex world out there, 'Father, have you been here all these years and said nothing?'

Ana could barely control her temper, 'You said it was no more than a chance recollection, Father, and I now discover you to be an expert!' This was worrying; that he should keep something hidden from her and in doing so had lied. But she would return to that later. At this moment she wanted to hear Gabriel's astonishing news. She crossed her fingers willing Gabriel to speak the truth. 'You say you were with my brother? This is an amazing claim.'

'My lady, I was his tutor for several years; then a few months ago we were reunited for a short while.'

'His tutor? Goodness me; this story grows more fanciful by the minute; and in what did you tutor him?'

'His language studies: French, Italian, German. I also taught him fencing and equestrian skills.'

With a shrug of her shoulders, beginning to think that her own fairy tales were but a pale imitation of a story such as this, Ana replied, 'I suppose I have to believe you. You could teach languages, fencing, horsemanship, but not, I take it, sweet pastries?'

'No. my lady, it was the Mendoza's pastry chef who taught me. I had learned but the rudiments at Salamanca.'

'Of course, how silly of me to forget so quickly, that was where you met Father Miguel. But do tell me about my brother. I must first warn you that I am fairly well informed about my brother. Should I find any of your information to be untrue I shall have no hesitation in having you arrested as some impertinent impostor.'

'And so you should. However I willingly accept the challenge,' Gabriel bowed. 'Your brother Don Francisco de Mendoza was born in Granada. It is a little known fact that during the months that your mother was with child she had an insatiable desire for raspberries and it is said that because of this Don Francisco carries the raspberry birthmark low down on his neck.'

'I know of this,' Ana interjected; long ago Blas had given her this information in his detailed report, 'go on.'

'Francisco was left with some people in the fiefdom of the Mendoza family who lived in a secluded area in the Alpujarras, the foothills of the Sierra Nevada, not far from the city of Granada. Not long afterwards he was abducted by the Moors, a not unusual occurrence in those days in that area. It was the lot of the kidnapped either to be sold into slavery or ransomed for a significant price. The Mendoza family lost no time in finding the ransom.'

Still suspicious Ana interrupted once more, 'I am not convinced, for there are several who know of this.'

'Then I shall remind you of an incident that very few know of. It took place here, in this very room, three or four years ago; your companions will vouch for it. A young maiden came here begging for something belonging to Ana de Jesus that she might take it to Santiago to have it blessed. You told your companions that you had had enough of beggars and they should send her away. The young girl tried once more saying that even a small piece of bread would suffice; and that was what you finally offered.'

Louisa gasped, 'I remember that day as if it were yesterday. My lady, I asked you to say something to the girl but you said you refused to speak to someone who would not show her face preferring to keep it hidden behind a fan.'

'How did you know of this Señor Gabriel?' Ana, reminded of that day and her behaviour, felt uncomfortable.

'Because I have seen the morsel of bread; it is lovingly kept on a small velvet cushion in an equally small gold casket.'

'Someone obviously wishes to remind themselves of my lack of Christian charity.'

'No, someone wishes to remind himself of his sister.'

Ana put her head in her hands in dismay, 'Dear God in Heaven, what did I do? I was so angry; angry with the condessa, angry with my Lady Aunt Magdalena, angry with beggars, angry with the world. But that is no excuse; I remember Louisa and Maria doing their utmost to persuade me to be generous while I continued to be stubborn. I drove away my brother, my own flesh and blood.'

'My lady, do not distress yourself, you were not to know. He was in disguise, he had no option, King Philip was and remains to this day fearful that there are those seeking to usurp his power in Portugal or Flanders, and to his mind Don Francisco being the son of Don Juan could well be one of them.'

'You fail to understand,' Ana wept, 'Despite my friends insisting they had noticed that the visitor's shoes were the shoes of a young man, that the fingers of his gloves had been cut away to allow for a larger hand, I continued in my obstinacy. How can I let him know how desperately sorry I am, how bitterly I regret squandering an opportunity to be with him?'

'I can get word to him, and rest assured that the day will come when you will, by God's good grace, be together again.'

Ana dried her tears, 'All my life I have invented make-believe stories as a way to escape these prison walls. At one time I actually believed that I might marry an Italian prince and go to live far away but that came to nought. I wonder if I dare to hope that this time … ?'

Father Miguel, still unnerved by Gabriel's unwitting revelations about his undercover activities and desperate for a speedy end to this interview, was quick to suggest they engage the *pastelero* asserting that this would make contacting her brother so much easier.

Ana raised a cautionary hand, she still knew little about this stranger. 'I think not so fast. For the moment I have two more questions. Señor, assuming you do have command of several languages, were they learned in your father's home or in a monastery?'

'Not in a monastery, as far as I know; nor can I say in my family home since I have no recollection of that either.'

'You are quite a mystery Señor Gabriel de Espinosa. What do you remember before becoming this expert tutor?'

'I remember regaining consciousness one cold starry night in a desert in Morocco. I was with a fellow soldier in King Sebastian's army, Cristobal, a comrade who has since become my closest and dearest friend; before that I know nothing.'

'You were with King Sebastian fighting the Turk?'

'Apparently so; how I got there and where from, I have no idea.'

'And yet, Father Miguel, you expect me to take someone with so vague a background into my household?'

'My lady, the time has come for me to end my silence. It is true that this gentleman has no idea of his background because that part of his memory was destroyed when he was so very badly wounded, but his friend Cristobal and I both know there is undeniable evidence that he is none other than King Sebastian of Portugal.' The vicar turned towards Gabriel and bowed, 'Forgive me, your majesty, but I had to tell.'

Chapter 13

The following morning saw Ana and the vicar walking in the cloister. The early August sun hadn't yet found enough strength to warm the cold stones of the cloister, nor to send folk seeking some shelter from its fierce rays.

Ana shivered, but it wasn't the chill of the air that was the cause. Her night had been hours of torment and her continued bewildered state gave her no peace. She was stunned by her ignorance that had come crashing in on her without warning. There could be no rest until she discovered who Father Miguel really was and what he was involved in. It had to be explained to her why there had been such secrecy and how many more secrets might there be. She also needed to know if she had been disgracefully arrogant towards her cousin, King Sebastian of Portugal; or, on the other hand, if he wasn't the king, who was he? Were these two men intent on deceiving her, and for what purpose?

Miguel followed hard on Ana's heels as she strode out across the flagstones to the central well. The moment she was seated on its parapet she launched into her rehearsed speech.

'I need explanations. Yesterday I was made to appear extremely foolish. I feel almost as if I have not been treading the same earth as you. I want you to make sense of this world I now find myself in, because I must tell you that I feel you have let me down very badly. Start by telling me who you are. All I know of you is that you were exiled from Portugal because of your support for Antonio, Prior of Crato, a contender for the throne, and that after years of exemplary behaviour in Salamanca you were sent here. That was years ago. Until yesterday I thought that was all I needed to know.' Her mouth had begun to twitch, her chin to tremble, she clasped her hands tight determined not to weep at what she considered to be callous treatment meted out by someone in whom she had had implicit trust.

'Allow me first to apologise for the lack of information about myself, although this is not unique. How much do you know of any priest, and that includes Brother Goldáraz, Doña Magdalena's Augustinian friend? But that is another story.'

'I agree, but matters have altered since yesterday's disclosure when our relationship was changed for ever.'

'Briefly, then, I was a court preacher in the employ of King Sebastian before taking up my duties as confessor to Don Antonio. I travelled with him to Morocco to fight alongside King Sebastian. We were captured being ransomed eventually by one of your kinfolk, the Princess of Eboli's son-in-law. Of course at that time everyone assumed King Sebastian to be dead so Don Antonio had become the desired heir to the throne. He was also recognised as the figurehead for Portugal's fight to maintain her independence from the enemy Castile. There had been others who had rights to the throne but they had been bought off by King Philip's agents; there is nothing like a hefty bribe for encouraging people to abandon their aspirations.'

'Quite; but I am not interested in them.'

'King Philip could barely contain his fury when he heard that Don Antonio was not only alive and well but was living in Castile. Despite the king's insistence that Don Antonio be held prisoner, he escaped to Portugal where he was greeted with open arms. The moment he was sworn in as king the soldiers of Castile were sent into Portugal, and King Philip set a reward of eighty thousand *ducados* for Don Antonio's head, so desperate was he to have the throne for himself.' Miguel had begun pacing to and fro, arms gesticulating wildly, his torrent of words becoming unintelligible.

'We will stop there for the moment. Do calm yourself, you look and sound like a hysterical crow jumping about some carrion. Sister Leonor, the *key lady,* and her shadow *Sister Parrot,* Agustina, are lurking in the arcade no doubt hoping to hear some titbit of gossip and I have every intention of disappointing them. Here,' she unhooked her Book of Hours from its gold chain at her waist, 'find the Hours of the Virgin, pretend you are instructing me on something.'

'My lady, you should show some Christian charity towards Sister Leonor ...'

'I have charity enough but only for those who are deserving; may God forgive me for the way I treated my brother. Now, slowly, tell me about your knowledge of secret codes and the like.'

'Don Antonio escaped Philip once again and made it to France. I have maintained contact with him over the years. Our correspondence is always in code or its equivalent, but I assure you it is for no other reason than we wish our letters to remain private. It is true that I have learned about various ciphers: those using numbers, or methods of substituting letters, or cleverly arranged musical notation. Invisible ink was yet another method I discovered. I have done nothing more in my letters than reiterate to my sovereign lord that he has my continued respect and honour ...'

'Ah, sisters,' Ana called across the cloister to the approaching nuns, 'what a beautiful part of the day this is, before the sun grows too hot to be borne.'

'Your Excellency,' Sister Leonor squeezed the words through her teeth and offered a minimum bending of the knees.

'... Excellency,' echoed the little devotee making a similar half curtsey.

'This has arrived,' Sister Leonor's bony fingers relinquished a letter.

Ana put it in the pocket of her robes. 'My goodness, but the *correo* must have been riding all night to get here so early, unless he arrived yesterday and the letter has been lying, ignored perhaps, on a table somewhere. Would you care to join us? Father Miguel has just been telling me of a legend about this illustration of the Holy Mother of God; see, this one.' She removed the book from the hands of the amazed priest. 'Here is the Virgin, exactly as it is mentioned in the Apocalypse, with the sun behind her and the crescent moon at her feet. Evidently Emperor Augustus; you did say it was Augustus? Yes, Emperor Augustus had a vision similar to this which made him decide not to become a god after all, but become a Christian instead.'

'All very interesting I am sure, but nuns about their daily duties have no time for such wasteful story telling; come, Sister Agustina.'

'... no time for wasteful ...' echoed Agustina scurrying after her.

Father Miguel shook his head at the smiling Ana, 'My lady I would not wish to accuse you of being devious, but really ...'

'She is a dangerous enemy, so I do or say whatever is necessary to protect myself from such a foe. You were saying that your letters to Antonio are to show your continued respect and devotion, nothing more, no suggestion of a Portuguese uprising?'

'Certainly not, for that would be treason against King Philip.' He looked about him then whispered, 'For several years now I have had a recurring vision of King Sebastian kneeling before an enormous crucifix. His green banner lies at his side, he holds aloft his general's baton in dedication. Nearby stands the Virgin, smiling her contentment. Then one day, as you know, in the monastery I saw him, I met King Sebastian. He was there before me. The visions continued until this same gentleman arrived here in Madrigal. Then they stopped. I need no further convincing; Gabriel de Espinosa is King Sebastian.'

Ana stood up, this was what she had been hoping to hear, afraid to hear. The pulse in her throat almost choked her, 'How can you be so sure?'

'He has the Hapsburg colouring: eyes, hair, skin, the telling trace of a limp in his left leg; the Thomas Aquinas book fastened to his belt. I must add some further, crucial information, the complete lack of evidence of King Sebastian's death. King Philip was desperate to have the remains of all the Royal House of Avis brought together – all dead and accounted for – and interred in Monastery of Belem in Lisbon, thus making it clear that no one stood between him and his legitimate claim to the Portuguese throne. However, he lacked the remains of King Sebastian. Some ashes, supposedly those of the presumed dead king, had been taken to from Alcazarquivir to Ceuta a few months after the famous battle. Four years, I repeat four years, were to elapse before these ashes were brought to Spain. The Princess of Eboli's son-in-law was then commanded to accompany them to Lisbon. The task was finally completed in 'eighty-two, according to King Philip. Now, if more proof is needed that King Sebastian is still alive and someone else's ashes are interred in Lisbon his friend Cristobal will furnish it.'

Ana's fears of yesterday were replaced by new and greater ones. No longer were there any unanswered questions. Now she was convinced that the stranger she met yesterday was the king of Portugal. What was she to do? She was getting involved in ... what? She needed time to think.

'I am off to visit Sister Isabel,' she did her utmost to look and sound light hearted. 'I must tell my dear friend that the hero of one of my childhood's bedtime tales has finally galloped into my fairytale land to rescue his Princess Maria, my beautiful doll.'

But how much dared she confide in dear Isabel? She had no wish to worry her ailing friend.

Chapter 14

Ana's salon sparkled with the light from dozens of candles: some in silver candlesticks others by their twos and threes in candelabra on the serving tables, while yet more in sixes and eights stood proudly atop their floor-standing candelabra. It was all so wonderfully extravagant to fill the room with so much golden warmth on this chilly and grey October evening.

Sisters Louisa, Maria and a newcomer to their happy little group, Sister Mencía, added to the cheer of the room with their gasps of surprise, with their laughter.

Ana looked down the length of the table her eyes passing over a trail of dessert debris on the white cloth: crumbs from pastries and almond cakes; scraps of marzipan and biscuits; dishes with oblongs of candied egg yolks; baked custards with their fruit purees, small glasses with traces of chocolate.

And there, at the far end sat her cousin King Sebastian. It was nothing short of a miracle; those years of prayer, the countless votive candles, all had played their vital part in protecting his life. It was a life so worthy of protection; everything Cristobal had told her confirmed this. Determined to fulfil his penance, which often put his safety or life at risk, Sebastian had always ensured that he, his close friend and kindred spirit, would never be in any danger.

This evening was another opportunity to be in his presence, to be enchanted again by that wonderful voice, to hear more of his adventures – so very different from those her dearest Isabel ever invented. She took her dear friend's hand in hers, saddened by its continued coldness, one of the many signs of a growing frailty. Isabel turned towards her and they exchanged smiles.

Father Miguel completed a tour of the table seeking to replenish empty wine glasses.

'This is how an evening should be spent,' announced Ana, 'with good food, good wine and most decidedly with good friends.'

Glasses were raised to the new Ana. Since the day the stranger had arrived in their midst her beauty had re-emerged from behind a sad and wasted complexion, her blue eyes twinkled with excitement, her curls – and this evening her wimple was pushed back further than ever to reveal more of them – shone their pure gold. The diamond brooches pinned to her bodice, her necklace and bracelets of emeralds and diamonds made her look even prettier than ever, almost leading the observer to forget that the black satin dress was, in fact, her nun's habit.

But there was no one, not even her closest friends, who could ever begin to understand how she felt; how could she expect them to when it was impossible to describe her emotions to herself. Her cousin, her very own cousin, was here with her. Here was the nephew of King Philip which meant they shared the same uncle. And he had met her brother. There was a warmth hitherto unknown that was flooding the whole of her being and she was happily drowning in it.

Isabel teased, 'By good friends does that also include Fortuna?' she asked, scooping some cream from a bowl for the lap dog to lick from her fingers.

'Why, of course it does,' Ana stroked the little darling sitting so comfortably in her lap waiting eagerly for any other treat that might come her way.

Father Miguel was about to sit down when there was an impatient rapping on the door. Without a pause it was pushed open and Sisters Leonor and Agustina stepped inside to stand statue-like before them. Leonor's eyes – whose hardened stare would certainly be enough to curdle the leftover cream – having first registered the guests and where they were seated, examined the serving board with its remains of roast lamb on a bed of apples, the chicken pieces in almond sauce. They then moved on to take an inventory of what was on the table: the custards, the *Tarta de Santiago*, the biscuits, candied eggs, the glasses of wine. Finally they took stock of the number of candles blazing merrily as if there were no tomorrow.

Ana came to welcome them, 'Roderos, chairs for our guests.'

'You are most kind, but we have eaten; boiled goat! Good enough for any servant of God! I simply came to advise you that I am about to lock the door should you have any guests from without the convent.'

'... from without the convent,' echoed Agustina.

Ana gave the unfortunate *Sister Parrot* a sympathetic smile. 'I insist you sit down. Señor Gabriel de Espinosa is about to entertain us. Roderos, some wine for the Sisters.'

Sister Leonor covered her glass with an impenetrable barrier of rigid fingers, 'Not a drop of wine will pass my lips while God is good enough to provide me with water.'

'... provide me with water,' Agustina was swift to follow her mentor's directives, although more than a hint of hesitation had crept into her voice and fingers.

Louisa had no intention of allowing Leonor to sour the mood of the occasion. 'Señor, do please tell us about one of your sea battles.'

'Very well; tonight I shall tell you of the time we saved three merchant ships from the thieving Turkish corsairs.'

They all, all that is, excepting Leonor and Agustina, leaned towards their favourite raconteur eager for him to begin.

The *pastelero* set the scene describing the azure sky and waters of the Mediterranean, painting a vivid picture of the galleasses with their fifty-six oars setting out from Messina to intercept pirates intent upon seizing the Spanish cargo of gold, silver, chocolate, sugar, and many other luxuries bound for the Kingdom of Naples.

'I saw it as a duty to assist the people of Naples and to demonstrate to the Turk that they did not have the freedom to tyrannise anyone venturing across that sea, to murder honest and innocent merchants going about their business.'

'You are so right,' agreed Maria.

'We had just passed the southern point of Sardinia when we caught sight of our quarry. Our oarsman pulled harder than ever and we soon closed with them. Unlike galleons once upon each other galleasses and galleys are locked together in battle, unable to move away, committed, until eventually one emerges as the victor.'

The tranquil scene of scarlet-bladed oars dipping and rising casting a myriad of diamond droplets across the blue waters, the bellied sails so proudly bearing the king's colours, was now to be replaced.

Gabriel went on, 'The quiet was shattered by the roar of cannon, the hiss of balls of iron or fire, the splintering and crashing of masts and spars. Those proud sails were ripped, burned, or fell lifeless about the decks or into the sea. Then to this din the men added their bellicose shouts as they leapt from one deck to another or stood ready to defend, determined to kill rather than be killed. Their screams and yells accompanied the cut and thrust of clashing sabre and scimitar. Have no fear ladies I shall spare you further details.'

He sipped at his wine then laughed, 'Had you been aboard that day you would not have believed your eyes when you came face to face with the enemy. Apart from their helmets that look for all the world like golden casserole covers the Turks wear the strangest and fullest of breeches; probably having as much cloth in them as a ship's sail, and these breeches are gathered at the ankle as a chemise sleeve is gathered at the wrist. Yes, there is a huge cuff at the ankle, and this is often adorned with gold or silver bands. Speaking of chemises, many of the Turkish soldiers preferred to dispense with them entirely wearing only a sleeveless leather doublet for protection. Then there were the jewels about their necks, chests, ears; I never saw so much adorning a man's person. The reason being that they would much rather carry all their booty from previous acts of piracy on their bodies than risk leaving it at home in the hands of others.'

Maria mocked, 'So much for honour among thieves! But what a splendid picture you paint. One question, if I may, what do the oarsmen do all the while this fighting is going on?'

'That depends on the captain. Normally they remain chained to their benches, but there are times when they are offered their freedom if they are prepared to fight the enemy. Our oarsmen were Spanish prisoners and there would be no doubting their loyalty so the captain freed them, an excellent way to put an end to the years of suffering deplorable conditions.'

Sister Leonor observed, 'To my mind they were reaping the just rewards of their evil actions and once the king had decided upon the punishment it should not be altered by anyone neither for any reason nor purpose.'

'... reason nor purpose,' echoed the *Parrot*.

Leonor gave her a withering look.

Ana clapped her hands to bring an end to the serious turn of the conversation, 'Tell us what happened after the fighting, what became of the Turks and your merchant vessels?'

'We had won the day; we took our enemies in chains back to Naples, we confiscated their galleys, and we stood to as our three galleons sailed by safely on her way. They had navigated their way across the Atlantic beating off storm, tempest and Queen Elizabeth's shameless English pirates, and we had seen them safely escape the Turk. The sailors lined up from bow to stern to cheer us.'

Ana held Isabel's still cold hands, 'I feel as though we were there instead of waiting in our palaces for our warrior princes to return as was the way in our childhood stories. We were never very good at imagining their tales of daring do, were we, Isabel?'

Isabel smiled remembering those bedtime stories, 'I suppose they did lack quite a bit when it came to the action, but then you were always in a hurry for the prince to come home, marry the princess and live happily ever after. Would you excuse me, I do feel rather tired.'

Gabriel stood to plead with her, 'Not yet awhile Sister Isabel, I promise not to detain you long but you must hear of my visit to Bethlehem, I should have told you of it instead of the sea battle. Sister Isabel I have been to the Holy Sepulchre.'

The room was filled with gasps of wonder and envy.

'First I had to pass through the church with its marble columns and mosaics before going down a staircase leading from the choir to a cave. This cave is lighted by thirty-two lamps. At the far end is a recess and under the altar there is a sign made of glittering stones saying *Hic de Virgine Maria Jesus Christus natus est.*'

They all made the sign of the cross.

'I went down another three steps to the chapel of the manger. The present manger is made of marble; the original one of wood is now in Rome, the new pope insisted on having it. However, the new manger stands on the place where the Christ child lay, and I worshipped where once the three Magi stood when they paid homage to Our Lord.'

After a moment's silence heavy with reflection Isabel moved painfully from her chair, 'Bless you, señor, I can take these precious images with me to my bed and to my rest, not only tonight but every night until I die. Ana is this not the best bedtime story of all time?'

'Yes, dear Isabel it is. Roderos will you and Dorotea help Sister Isabel to her room. I shall join you in a moment.'

Leonor and Agustina were already on their way out; Leonor too impatient to wait until they were out of earshot for the venom to flow, 'Mark my words no good will come of this! A ne'er do well seated at the head of the table of a princess telling second hand stories picked up from goodness knows where. But he spins a good yarn. Whether there is any truth in anything he says is another matter, he has a clever mind and an equally clever tongue. What I can tell you is that without a shadow of doubt that man is no *pastelero*. That man is in disguise, a rogue.'

'... in disguise, a rogue. How right you are Sister, the man is patently an impostor.'

Leonor had no time to recover from the shock of Agustina speaking for herself, there was yet more to come.

Agustina hurried on, 'What I do regret is denying myself the chance to try a biscuit dipped in a glass of that delicious looking chocolate. Now I can only wonder if I will ever have another opportunity or whether its delights are lost to me for ever.'

Chapter 15

Ana shut the door behind the retreating nuns, pausing for a moment, Leonor's words echoing, threatening. What could she possibly say to that dreadful woman that might come anywhere close to excusing her unconventional behaviour towards Sebastian without revealing his identity?

Could she perhaps intimate that he was of a high ranking family but that within that family a feud had led to violence, a death perhaps, and that despite his innocence there were still those who accused, causing him to ... what? It was a slippery slope once you began to employ falsehoods. But should she ignore her conscience if by what she said or did was to protect her beloved cousin?

Dorotea saved her from further soul searching, 'My lady, Sister Isabel is in her bed, but says that before sleeping she would dearly like to speak with you.'

'I shall go immediately. Would you have the table cleared and the cushions on the dais plumped up? Ask Roderos to place two chairs nearby for Father Miguel and the *pastelero*.'

The folly of her ways was brought home to her once more; she was directing her servants to arrange the room to accommodate a common tradesman. They would never query her actions; all the same something must be done, this couldn't be allowed to continue.

Isabel was reclining amongst her many pillows, her hands resting on the luxurious blue velvet quilt that had been tucked about her.

'It was the best decision you could have made, my friend, agreeing to return to live in my apartments. You look stronger as each day passes.'

'That is as may be, my princess, but that is not what I wish to talk about. Here, sit by me,' Isabel patted the quilt.

Like a dutiful child Ana sat on the edge of the bed.

'I shall be brief,' Isabel explained before rushing through a swift resume of Ana's history. 'We both know how unkind life has been to you: sent here as a tiny child; held here despite your complete lack of vocation; still bound to the convent even when acknowledged as the king's niece; the offer of a most favourable marriage denied you. We are also both painfully aware that your loyalty to our king, your uncle, can never be questioned; that only at his death and the accession of his son will you seek your liberty.'

'You have no idea how often I contemplate the growing ill health of King Philip, how often I think of that letter in Father Miguel's safekeeping ready and waiting to be sent to His Holiness.'

'Oh, but I have. However, I want to talk about romance. Eventually, when your freedom becomes a reality, you may wish to spend the rest of your life with your beloved cousin, King Sebastian.'

'Isabel, such thoughts have never crossed my mind!'

'Really? Then my eyes and ears must be deceiving me these days.' Isabel giggled mischievously, 'Fortunately by then there will be very few of your relatives left who may still feel it their right to determine your future; and not one priest would dare insist in taking charge, knowing how the clergy disobeyed the spirit and the law of the Council of Trent allowing you to be incarcerated here. In fact, the way I see it, you will be in a position to make your own decisions. At last one of your fairy tales will come true.'

'If only that were possible; whenever I have dared to imagine a future beyond these walls my plans have always come to a halt. I am sure I could never withstand the pressures that will still exist to have me remain here, to deny me the right to marry despite my wealth.'

'Believe me you will overcome any obstacle presented; you have the same courage and determination as the young lady I heard of a few years ago. I want you to take heed of this story it will stand you in good stead.'

'I will be guided by you as always my dear friend and mentor.'

Isabel raised an admonishing finger, 'This is no time to mock. The lady I refer to was very young, very rich, and a widow. Within months of her husband's demise her father died without a male heir leaving her his vast fortune to add to her already considerable wealth. There was such a scurrying about by executors and priests to either marry her off or have her retire to a convent, and of course her darling son would have to be raised by some tutor or other — to be sure a young lady would never be capable of attending to her own affairs especially when so much money and power was involved, only men have such an ability. Over the following months she used as many delaying tactics as she could, frustrating all the preying pests beyond words, then the war against Portugal conveniently came along concentrating most folks' minds and her status was put to one side. God works in mysterious ways because within months two of the executors were removed from the scene. One of them, the king's secretary Perez, was imprisoned. He was involved in more skulduggery than you would believe possible.'

'Perez; ah yes, Blas told me about him and his affair with the Princess of Eboli, and how she used him to decipher coded letters from Portugal because she wanted information to help support the rights of someone in her family to the Portuguese throne. Treason!'

'Do not tire me with digressions. As I said, two executors, the most powerful, were removed from the scene, one being Perez; the other, an abbot, who unfortunately died of influenza. Nothing happened for some time then without warning came the news, the lady had married! *Fait accompli*; goodness me, there was such consternation and all to no avail.'

'So it is possible.'

'Of course it is. What you must do is this; make your commitment to King Sebastian immediately then have him curtail his visits here. It is no longer safe for you or him, not with the likes of Leonor and her vile opinions and her determination to meddle; may God forgive me for my unkindness. I would go so far as to say that it is best he leaves Madrigal forthwith to continue his search for penance, while you learn to endure a few more years of loneliness until that happy day arrives when you can be together.'

'You never cease to amaze me.'

Isabel brushed the compliment aside, 'That is all I have to say on the matter. God bless you my child; goodnight, and do close the door on your way out.'

When Ana returned to the salon her head was still spinning with Isabel's advice and thoughts of the dangerous Leonor.

'May I speak, my lady?' a now serious Sebastian greeted her and led her to the dais where her friends rose to curtsey.

'I doubt any of your words can return us to the earlier pleasures of this evening.'

'No, they cannot. My lady, knowledge of my presence in Madrigal has travelled through Spain and has reached Portugal,' Sebastian gave Miguel an accusing glance whose hands emerged from his cavernous black sleeves to deny any involvement. 'As the weeks pass more and more riders arrive at my door to humble themselves and to yield their tithes insisting they are my vassals. In a town of this size such comings and goings cannot go unnoticed for long. My visits here will eventually be connected in some way. This evening has made it abundantly clear that something must be done. I certainly cannot come again, and I should seriously plan my departure from Madrigal; apart from all else I am beginning to neglect my penance.'

'Oh dear, no! You cannot leave us.' chorused Louisa, Maria, and Mencía.

Ana looked bleakly at him. She might wish to dismiss the riders as nothing other than messengers sent to make enquiries about the exquisite pastries but it was true his visits here were foolhardy, connected or not with these riders. From everything she had heard she gathered that suspicions were rampant in Castile aggravated by a number of problems: the king was ailing; he no longer had his favourite advisers; there was political unrest; famines and financial crises were a perennial threat. These days anyone could stand accused of any misdemeanour. She was related to the king, a relation forced to live in seclusion; this could cause additional problems for Sebastian. Inexplicably everything was suddenly becoming complicated. Sebastian must leave; this was the unavoidable, inevitable, brutal conclusion she herself had arrived at only minutes ago.

Sebastian continued, 'It did not escape Sister Leonor's notice that I sat at the head of the table.'

Louisa argued, 'But that is because it is all part of a fairy tale tableau come to life.'

'I am afraid Sister that after a lifetime of make-believe it is time for you to dismiss such childish fantasies, comforting though they may be. It is time to be realistic. Sister Leonor saw where I was sitting and that Father Miguel bowed his head whenever he addressed me. We are entering difficult territory.'

Miguel's hands emerged once again from his black sleeves on this occasion to flap apologies, his words tumbling forth in an increasingly heavy Portuguese accent. 'My behaviour can be easily explained to anyone who asks. It came about quite by accident. Sire, I will say that you reminded me so much of my former sovereign, that I lost myself in those happy days at the court in Lisbon. But on another topic, that of your leaving, that is out of the question because God has spoken to me of His grand design. He says you and Ana must marry and await the moment when He will call you to the Portuguese throne ...'

Sebastian cut him short, 'Please, no more of this nonsense. I have spoken to you about this many times and this is to be the last. The cause of the decline of Portugal lies heavily on King Sebastian. He chose through arrogance to lead thousands to Morocco to their untimely and squalid deaths leaving hundreds of families decimated. If I am that man I must carry that burden on my soul and twenty years of penance could never be enough to assuage such guilt. If, on the other hand, I was one of his ardent followers then I am equally culpable, standing accused for the heavy loss of compatriots' lives and family fortunes, for the eventual selling off of Portugal to Spain by a section of snivelling nobility who had remained at home and were only too eager to snap up Spanish bribes. I pray that my years of penitence and remorse, whoever I am, will go some way to mitigate my part in all this. What I want to make absolutely clear is that once my penance is completed I intend to retire far from the ugly face of politics, I have seen and heard enough never to want to be a part of it again. As for Portugal, the Royal House of Avis is finished, but with the Royal House of Braganza to lead her one day she will once again determine her own future.'

Those earlier precious images of adventures on the high seas, of visits to the place of Christ's birth were now as nothing. Sebastian's audience had been silenced.

'I beg you to forgive my boldness,' he went on. 'I have only one desire in life and that is for Your Excellency to join me in my retirement.' He went down on his knees before Ana.

Without a moment's hesitation she replied. 'I shall be here waiting for you and when King Philip is no more I will be honoured to become your wife. Father Miguel would you be so good as to perform a betrothal ceremony this very moment? We have witnesses enough.'

It was resolved as easily as that.

Father Miguel was delighted since it suited his plans perfectly; there would be a king and queen for Portugal after all, despite Sebastian's protestations. Ana's friends sighed with joy at the romance of it all. Ana was convinced it was the only decision she could possibly have made. All she wanted was to marry the man she loved and there was no denying she loved him with all her heart and nothing would bring her greater happiness than to spend her life with him.

Sebastian put his hand to his heart, 'My lady, I am honest and reliable. Although I lack status, in Italy I have income enough to keep you in luxury. But more than this I love and honour you. I know you seek a family life, wanting to be loved and cherished, and to love and cherish in return. We can do this together.'

Ana took his hands in hers and raised him. Her breath caught in her throat, the words would not come easily. She was nervous; the enormity of her decision was beginning to overwhelm her. She stumbled awkwardly through her speech. 'If by status you mean being of noble birth; that holds no interest for me whatsoever, heaven knows I have had enough experience of those people to last a lifetime. My lord, I do believe you to be King Sebastian but am quite happy to ignore that fact; for me it is your compassion for your fellow man and your unsurpassed loyalty that commend you to me and cause me to love you.'

They kissed hands as Ana's friends gathered round giggling with excitement.

Following the short ceremony Miguel addressed his small congregation, 'It is most fitting that at this point our thoughts should be directed towards the god Cupid.'

'Why, yes, of course,' Louisa replied, 'the god of love, but at this religious moment? Is that not a kind of blasphemy?' She crossed herself.

'I may be considered strange, perhaps, but not in the least blasphemous that we find ourselves in the presence of gods and goddesses of love as well as the Almighty Father. Things are not always as they seem. Cupid offered Harpocrates a rose as an inducement never to reveal the activities of his mother Venus and that is where we find the connection. Have you noticed the carved roses over the confessionals?'

They nodded.

'Exactly, they are there because they signify the secrecy and confidentiality of confession – under the rose – *sub rosa*. What we have witnessed this evening is also *sub rosa* and to be guarded as jealously as any word heard in sacramental confession or as any of the secrets of Venus.'

Louisa clapped her hands, 'Roses and gods of love and secrecy, it reminds me of those wonderful bedtime stories when we were children! Oh, I know we should put behind us all those happy lands of daydreams, but just this once I hope to be excused.'

'And we need an exchange of gifts between the betrothed,' Maria insisted, 'in our stories happy couples always exchanged gifts.'

Ana blushed, 'You are so right.' She removed the ring from her forefinger, a silver ring with a single emerald stone which refused to fit any of Sebastian's fingers.

He then offered an ivory ring from his little finger, a ring that would never be secure on any of Ana's.

'No matter,' she laughed hurrying from the room. Within seconds she was back with a small casket.

Inside was a nest of chains. Ana carefully selected three. The rings were slid onto two of them and Ana and Sebastian slipped them over their heads. The third chain held a locket.

'I wanted you to have this some time ago but there was never a right moment.' Ana laughed, 'You can see that I have done more for you than I would ever consider doing for the prioress.'

Sebastian opened the locket and there, facing a miniature portrait of his betrothed was a lock of her beautiful blond hair. He kisses her cheeks whispering, 'My love, my life,' and Ana fell into his arms.

'My brother could never have imagined any of this when he sent you to me.'

'But he will be delighted when I tell him.'

'You will visit him?'

'Of course I will. Oh, my dear, sweetest Ana, I hate to have to leave you, and so suddenly but there is no alternative. The sooner I put some distance between us the safer you will be from idle or mischievous gossip.'

Ana nodded her acceptance, determined to be positive.

'Cristobal will not be accompanying me; he will remain with his wife and child. And there will be some consolation in this for you. He will visit the *locutorio*. You know how much he resembles me, so this could prevent further tongue-wagging amongst the nuns and Leonor will have the satisfaction that we have taken notice of her complaints. Cristobal will deliver pastries and bring you news of me. I think, too, if he were to bring his two year old daughter you would find in her the most pleasurable of company.

'My lord, you think of everything,' Ana was determined to stay cheerful. 'Isabel said that only a few years of your penance remain, and I could surely endure a little extra loneliness, knowing we would eventually be together. Dare I dream such dreams?'

Louisa and Maria insisted, 'You must, you must!'

'Then I shall!'

Chapter 16

Ana welcomed the two nuns into her salon with the happiest, the most contented of smiles.

In return Leonor and Agustina peered with a studied coldness at the scene before them. Ana and a young child were seated on footstools at a makeshift table fashioned from a small chest. Ana's doll also had a setting at the table opposite the little girl, and she stood supported by chair legs and a cushion.

'I am afraid you have arrived too late for the banquet, for as you see we are almost finished.'

The silver dishes and bowls held only the merest scraps of chopped chicken in frumenty and a dessert of quince jelly angel hair.

'But allow me to introduce ourselves. I am Queen Paciencia and these are my daughters the Princesses Esperanza and Consuela,' Ana indicated the child and the doll.

At the mention of her name the little two year old put down her horn cup to stand and curtsey to the nuns.

This Princess Esperanza, or Clara Eugenia, to give her her real name was Cristobal's daughter who had so quickly become the child Ana had earnestly longed for. She would spend hours concocting new games, pastimes, all kinds of diversions to keep them both occupied. For the past half hour or so they had been playing a game of queens and princesses and it would be difficult for an observer to determine who was enjoying it most.

Ana gently caressed the child's head and began, 'The queen and princesses lived in a big, high tower.'

Ana and Clara reached up as high as they could, Clara following closely Ana's every movement.

'They lived in this big, high tower for years.'

Again their hands shot up into the air and this time the little dog Fortuna stood on her hind legs making Clara laugh.

'They had been waiting for news of the king but had heard nothing.'

Ana and Clara looked at each other and shook their heads.

'So, today they have decided to send out a messenger. Princess Esperanza,' Clara stood to curtsey at the sound of her name, 'has written the letter. Do show it to our visitors.'

'Yes, Mama,' Clara picked up her practice sheet with its rows of pink, vertical lines over which she had executed some that were very black and wobbly. She carried her morning's effort to the nuns for their inspection.

Ana continued, 'After their siesta they will seal the letter and give it to the messenger. There is enough money to pay. Shall we count it out?' She handed Clara a drawstring purse, 'Are you ready?'

Clara counted, 'One, two, three.'

Ana hugged her, 'How clever you are.' Ana forced her attention away form the darling in her care to the face of Leonor. It was a picture of disdain and fomenting anger, although why, Ana couldn't fathom for children were such a joy.

'But now they are tired, it is time to go to their bedchamber to sleep on large, round, plump pillows.'

Clara imitated Ana's sweeping, circling arm movements then picked up Ana's doll, made two circuits of the room with the excited Fortuna about her heels and climbed the steps of the dais to the awaiting cushions.

Ana planted kisses on her petal-soft cheeks before accompanying the nuns to the door.

Once in the gallery she asked, 'To what do I owe the pleasure of your company, Sister Leonor?'

'We came to offer our condolences on the passing of Sister Isabel.'

'I thought we came to see who ...' Agustina sounded perplexed.

'Then you thought wrong!' snapped Leonor.

Ana reverently bowed her head, 'I thank you for your kind sentiments. Sister Isabel will be a great loss; she was a mother to me from the first day I came here. Yes, she will be irreplaceable, a more Christian soul we could never meet. God rest her soul,' she crossed herself. 'But what did you think of my precious guest, Clara Eugenia, is she not perfect?'

Leonor folded her arms and icily commented, 'I had no idea there was a noble family in the vicinity, not with so young a child.'

'That is correct; Clara Eugenia is the child of the *pastelero*.' She crossed her fingers behind her back, hoping God would ignore the deception. Cristobal, the father, was indeed a *pastelero*, but not the one that Leonor had met and would naturally assume to be the father in question.

'And does she have a mother?'

'Of course, a dear lady, Inez is her name. Perhaps you may meet her later when she comes to collect Clara. Is there any other information I could provide?'

'No, thank you; it was only a passing curiosity, nothing more.'

'... a passing curiosity, nothing more,' echoed Agustina.

Leonor waited until Ana had returned to her apartments before unleashing a deluge of jealousies and grievances. 'What is this convent coming to? Obsequiousness is rampant, people breaking their necks to be one of the chosen to sit at Her Excellency's table or to be one of the fawning recipients of the leftover scraps. There are far too many not content with convent fare, desperate instead for fine foods, nuts and fruits.' She whirled on Agustina, 'And you are no better than the rest, still pining over the biscuits and chocolate you never got to taste.'

'I simply commented ...'

'No excuses. Now we have this outrage. This little madam: perhaps two years old; nothing but the daughter of a tradesman; airs and graces of someone far above her station; eating from silver dishes and a napkin at her fingertips; learning to write and do her numbers. *Señorita Tal y Cual*, Little Miss So-and-So, that is who she is. I tell you this must be stopped; there is something evil lurking here. The Lord knows I have warned the prioress of the disturbing direction in which this kind of thing is leading us, but what does she do?'

'... what does she do? So far as I know she does nothing, but then she does not enjoy good health; and surely this is all rather harmless?'

'Until you can think of something sensible to say I suggest you say nothing at all! I shall send word to Goldáraz although I have little faith in him. His presence here might return us to some form of normality.'

Eager to atone for her errors in defending the innocent, Agustina thought she would hint at intrigue. 'Do you suppose anything was meant by Her Excellency when she was pretending they were going to send a message?'

There was a silence while the two conjured up various possibilities.

'Agustina, that is a good point, a very good point; you have definitely risen in my estimation. The *pastelero* never visits Ana's apartments, in fact he rarely comes the convent and then only into the *locutorio*. Ana must be writing to him!'

Agustina was delighted and decided to add more, 'Yes! And may I ask you to consider further the parentage of the child? I sense more mystery here,' she twinkled with excitement. 'First of all, the name Clara Eugenia; that is the name of our king's daughter, the Princess Isabel Clara Eugenia. Secondly, she looks very much like one of the Hapsburg family. I believe the father could be one of the following: Ana's uncle in Flanders; her brother Don Francisco; her cousin Archduke Alberto, present governor of Portugal; her cousin Prince Philip; even King Sebastian of Portugal, who may still be alive. And, no, let me finish,' she waved her arms to propel her through this flurry of fantasies, 'what if Ana is the child's mother? What if the *pastelero* used magic potions to seduce her and he is the father?'

Chapter 17

'Give some serious thought to my words,' Brother Goldáraz concluded, 'Doña Magdalena would not be best pleased, Your Excellency, if it were to come to her attention that you have allowed a common tradesman such liberties. I would also venture to suggest you reconsider the advisability of inviting the child into your private apartments. On both counts I would urge you to remember who you are and what you are.'

'Yes, Father,' Ana replied having neither the desire nor patience to argue with the old priest.

'So, I have your promise that you will have nothing more to do with *Señor Fulano,* Mister What's-His-Name, Espinosa. It is for the general good of my convent.'

'Yes, Father.' Ana nodded gravely, happy in the knowledge that Sebastian was in Navarre, and secretly amused that the truth had finally escaped Goldáraz; his concern was for his convent and not for her at all.

'Then I must be off to see the prioress. God bless you, my child.'

She watched him make his painful and tottering way along the gallery to disappear round the corner before permitting herself a sigh of relief. The questioning was over; she had told him everything she thought he ought to know about Gabriel de Espinosa, King Sebastian of Portugal and her betrothed. The priest had sounded either sympathetic or patronising, excusing her actions as those of an innocent with no experience of the wicked world beyond the convent walls. She had played her role quite well being less than honest at times, driven purely by circumstances, determined to convince the priest of her naïveté.

Nevertheless she was left angry and uneasy. Why had Goldáraz come to question her and why should she have to justify her behaviour? Why, in a convent of all places, should anyone concern themselves with somebody's status? How could it possibly harm her reputation? No one knew or cared about her existence, for goodness' sake! She was certain that he had come in response to the poisonous Sister Leonor. That was a worry, Leonor was evil personified and capable of saying and writing anything.

Sister Louisa joined her, 'He seemed satisfied enough?'

'Yes, but I shall have to continue to be vigilant especially where Leonor is concerned. What a ridiculous state of affairs! Thank goodness my darling Clara Eugenia will be here soon; balm enough for my troubled heart. And if anyone supposes that for one moment I should bring these visits to an end they are well and truly mistaken.

'I agree. But those are only a few, very few in fact, with no sense of proportion. I think it is nothing more than a case of idle minds or empty heads desperately searching for something exciting to fill the vacuum.'

'I thank God that all my letters were delivered before all this nonsense broke loose. Everything has been said that needed to be said. Only one letter is outstanding, and that is innocent enough, Cristobal's news of my brother. From now on we shall have to rely on our prayers for loved ones with only scant information finding its way here,' she fingered the chain about her neck with its ivory ring.

The bell announced an arrival at the convent door. 'That will be Clara. Hurry, we cannot keep her waiting.'

They raised their skirts to race down the staircase to be at the huge door as soon as it was pushed open.

Señora Inez and Clara Eugenia stood frozen in their tracks. In front of them a reception committee of nuns had gathered filling the doorway. Ana called to Clara and the nuns stepped aside.

The child was wearing the new dress that Ana had ordered to be made for her. It was of figured grey velvet with dainty pink roses, with a pink velvet bodice. A fine lawn collar sat perfectly at the neck. Ana forgave herself her indulgence; she had so wanted to have Clara wearing something that she would dearly have loved to have worn when she was a child. To complete the pretty picture Clara had a handkerchief, beautifully embroidered by Sister Mencía, hanging from the pink girdle at her waist. And, of course, she carried Ana's doll.

One of the nuns giggled, 'Step aside for the *Señorita Tal y Cual.*'

This set them all performing mock curtseys.

'And, would you believe it, a collar! Such an upstart family to dare to have their child wear a collar!'

Ana was quite restrained, 'Who is to say the child is not from a noble family? Many a person of rank has spent his or her youth in obscurity. This child one day could well be a benefactress of this convent, so it behoves us to moderate our words and actions.' She gathered Clara up into her arms and kissed her.

'Clara, what a pretty dress! So many roses!' Louisa pointed to some of the tiny flowers.

'Roses,' repeated Clara poking her finger first at one then another, 'Pink.'

'Pink roses; so they are! See what I have made for you, your favourite sweets.' Louisa handed her a paper cone filled with fudge.

Clara peeped inside the package, 'Thank you. May I save them today? May I keep them for my father until he comes back?'

Ana did not dare chance even the quickest of glances at Louisa. 'Has your father gone away, Clara?'

'Yes, but he is coming home soon. The sweets will be a gift for him.'

'Clara, Clara Eugenia!' The call was from Mencía as she ran along the arcade, 'How lovely you look in your new dress,' she panted. 'Now then what do you think of this? I made this little lady especially for you.' Mencía had to stop to catch her breath.

Ana set Clara down taking the sweets and pushing the doll deep into her pocket having felt the note hidden amongst its petticoats.

The nuns stopped their gossiping about the possible parentage of the child to stare in open-mouthed horror at Mencía, frantically crossing themselves.

'Dear God in Heaven; the Blessed Virgin Mary; heresy; witchcraft.'

Clara reached for the new doll, her very own. 'A nun, a nun just like you, all in black and white; look,' she said toddling off happily to show her new doll to Father Miguel who had emerged from the chapel and was making his way towards them.' I have a new doll, a nun. She looks like my friends.'

Miguel smiled down on her and patted her head, 'Who made it for you?'

'Sister Mencía. Oh, I forgot,' she went back to hug the nun's skirts. 'Thank you, Sister Mencía. My very own doll.'

The nuns stood in chilled silence, desperate to have Father Miguel gone, that they could share their indignation and fears about a nun daring make something that could possibly be, most probably was, perhaps, a witch's familiar.

'Shall we play a ball game?' Louisa took a feather filled ball from her pocket and threw it to Clara who dropped it then kicked it into the climbing roses just beyond her reach. She and Ana got down on their knees to retrieve it. But then Clara became far more interested in Ana's silver pomander on its silver chain. It was a beautiful ball, far prettier than the cloth one that was lost. She tried to throw it but the chain held it fast and it travelled no further than Ana's forehead.

Ana cried out, shocked, holding her hand to the injury while Clara wept repeating, 'Sorry, sorry, sorry.'

'It was nothing more than an accident,' Ana assured her.

Louisa and Mencía rushed to comfort them both.

The nuns were far too inquisitive to remain aloof from the commotion. They quickly gathered round just as Father Miguel spread his arms beaming paternally on Ana and Clara. He raised his eyes heavenwards and declared, 'Such a mother, such a daughter.'

Chapter 18

For the fifth or sixth time Imelda paced the floor of the poorly lit room, one of the best the inn had to offer, but gloomy nonetheless. What little light there was edged its way timidly through the window that opened on to the narrow gallery overlooking the courtyard.

Each step was becoming more agitated than the last and she pushed fitfully at her rolled-up sleeves. She stopped once more at the table lifting a silver plated dish close to her myopic eyes before hastily returning it to its exact position; she did the same with the spoon. Her next port of call was the simple chest in the corner where she checked the green velvet doublet and trunk hose ensuring the folds were unchanged after her inspection. A few strides brought her again to the bed; there was still nothing concealed under the straw mattress. The travelling bag did however have further items of good quality clothing amongst which was a letter. The letter might be of some importance.

Imelda approached the door to click her tongue in frustration, glaring at it for stubbornly remaining as closed as ever then turned to continue her repeated tour. At last she was stopped in her agitated pacing by the sounds of men's voices and footfalls on the staircase and outside gallery growing ever closer. Finally she was to have some company; she would no longer be alone. With shaking hands she adjusted her white linen cap and not-so-white apron.

Her husband held the door to allow a middle-aged portly gentleman in black and four accompanying armed guards to enter.

A swift bobbed curtsey and Imelda launched into a nervous babbling, 'I thanks the Lord you got here; I was scared he might be here first and me on me own; I mean what would I have done? I was beginning to think my husband should have stayed here while I …'

'Quite, quite; I take it you are the wife of this good man?' The short and rotund gentleman, Don Rodrigo de Santillán, removed his gloves and placed them gingerly on a closely scrutinised part of the table. He then rearranged his black robe at his shoulders, each finger enjoying the depth and luxurious silkiness of the fox fur reveres. This splendid article he had bought for himself as a reward for his diligence brought to the king's service as chief magistrate for the City of Valladolid.

'Your worship, this inn has been in the family for generations,' Imelda went on, 'and never a hint of shady business, never a brush with the law. We've always had a good reputation, we have. We have folk from all over Spain staying here, aye, and some from further afield to visit the stores and shops around here; the spices and silver …'

'Indeed, mistress; I know the city well, being its chief magistrate. But enough, I have been called here to be shown proof of your husband's accusations,' his deep and authoritative voice found its way into every nook and cranny of the chamber.

'Oh, there's that alright and plenty of it. I can assure you. Where do you want to start, your worship?'

'We shall start with you holding your tongue.' Santillán turned to the innkeeper, 'How do you tolerate such rantings; does she never stop?'

Pablo the innkeeper looked from the magistrate, to the armed guard, to his wife, and back to the magistrate offering the smile of a simpleton.

'So, tell me all about it.'

'Your worship, it was like this,' Pablo rubbed his hands up and down the sides of his breeches. He'd taken off his apron when he'd gone in search of the law and now had nothing to fidget with. 'The guest asked me to help him with the points to his trunk hose, they'd come loose and his shirt was sticking out from under his doublet.'

'Do get to the point.'

'Well he had this lovely silver chain around his neck with a locket kind of thing, and it was dangling outside his shirt because he hadn't fastened the collar yet.'

'Dear Lord in Heaven; get on with it. You saw a silver locket and chain.'

'And he showed me what was inside.' Pablo nodded his pride at having such a secret to be told to no one less than the magistrate himself. 'It was the picture of a beautiful lady and a dog. But guess what; when I asked if that was his wife he laughed and said she would never marry the likes of him, she would marry somebody important. He only worked for her.'

'Probably a gift from the lady, it is not unknown.'

'That's as may be, but wait for this. Next he shows me the ring on his little finger, and asks do I know whose likeness is on it. I says it is our master, King Philip. And what does he do? I'll tell you what he does; he shakes his head and says King Philip is my master but definitely not his! Now what do you think about that?'

'That is most interesting,' Santillán stroked his well trimmed black beard.

'So, as soon as he left I told Imelda about it and she said I shouldn't waste any time in telling you.'

'That's right,' agreed the innkeeper's wife, 'I says we are honest folk running an honest business and we want no nonsense here. I wants this man out and away!'

Santillán smiled at the idea of this inn being run as an honest business; if that were true it would be quite unique. He did, however, have some sympathy for this middle aged couple who were afraid they had stumbled upon something they saw as threatening to their livelihood. He could see how they were afraid that their innocent involvement could well invite his condemnation; and justifiably so, he was a powerful man!

'You did right to come to me. Of course this may be nothing more than folly, words spoken in jest; but it is best for you to protect yourselves.'

'And there's more,' Imelda couldn't remain quiet a moment longer, 'just take a look at these dishes and spoon; silver they are, my pewter's not good enough!'

Santillán picked up a bowl to inspect it.

Imelda hurried on, 'Stolen; that's what I thought, but I've changed my mind since I found something else. There's some funny business going on.'

She went to the travelling bag and brought the letter to thrust into the magistrate's hand.

'You truly have been busy, good woman.' He turned it over and examined the blood red seal bearing what might be a shield. He pursed his lips, put the letter down on the table tapping at it and wondering.

'*Your golden hair, my lass ... *' a rich, melodious voice was singing a folk song, somewhere close by, near the foot of the stairs.

'That's him,' Imelda grasped at her calloused elbows. 'Now you'll see.'

'*... it has me tied to you.*
Free me if it's nought to you.

'*Leave me to my complaining ...*' the singer stepped into the room.

He was a man in his forties; a tall man with fair hair. It was Cristobal de Silva. His singing had

136

been silenced by the reception committee. He was further puzzled by the presence of the four guards, two at either side of the door.

He determined to remain composed, 'Goodness me, seven of you here already leaving barely enough space for me. To what do I owe such a reception?'

'You will first remove your sword and hand it, along with your dagger, to my guards,' Santillán drew himself up to his full, though diminutive, height. 'I am the chief magistrate and I am here regarding the possibility of your involvement with theft. What is your name?'

'I am deeply shocked; there must be some grave misunderstanding.'
Cristobal turned to the innkeeper and his wife who refused to meet his eye.

'I repeat, señor, what is your name?' Santillán did not conceal his temper.

'With respect, your honour, knowing my name would neither increase nor decrease my guilt or innocence. I am known as the *Pastelero*.'

'Let us begin with the table ware.'

'They are mine and have been in my possession for about fifteen years. They are a gift from a duque whose name I will not divulge, it would be quite wrong to drag an innocent man into this sordid affair.'

Santillán was beginning to feel unsettled by this self-assured *pastelero*. 'Then what of the silver chain and locket, and the ring, what can you say about them?'

The *pastelero* gave a questioning look at the innkeeper who lowered his eyes, 'I would prefer not to discuss the locket; but what of the ring?'

'Tell him, master innkeeper.'

Pablo, rubbing his hands up and down his breeches, stammered, 'You said as how King Philip was not your master.'

'Ah, so I did. That was wrong of me, your honour. I was carried away by thoughts of my master, the king of Portugal, at the battle of Alcazarquivir; but that was long ago. Sometimes these memories take us unawares.'

'So you were a part of that disaster, were you? This man was a Portuguese soldier, fighting for King Sebastian. Did you understand that, innkeeper?'

Cristobal insisted, 'I never said I was Portuguese. I said I was in the Portuguese army.'

'You begin to annoy me,' Santillán observed. This man before him was handsome some may say with those big blue eyes and fair hair, and with interesting scars about his temples. This *pastelero* was also well spoken, stood tall and straight; he refused to give his own name as well as divulging those of others. Nor would he tell his nationality; it was all most strange. At first he thought he would be dealing with some petty felony, but now; well he was confused.

'This letter, señor pastry cook, was discovered amongst your belongings.'

'Ah, the letter; you have been most thorough.'

Santillán looked at Imelda who gently stroked her elbows with satisfaction before directing a smug look of victory at the *pastelero*.

'I refuse to say a word about the letter; at least not in public,' Cristobal was adamant.

'Then you leave me no choice. You will accompany me to my office.' Santillán picked up the letter and his gloves and moved towards the door.

'I thank you, your honour, for granting me this privacy.'

'I can assure you that this is not a cordial invitation. This is an order; indeed I am arresting you. Manacle this man.'

Imelda was swift to interrupt before any irons were placed about the *pastelero*'s wrists, 'What about you paying for tonight, and for the stabling of your horse?'

'Of course, Mistress Imelda,' Cristobal withdrew several coins from his purse, 'there should be sufficient here for a few evenings, have no fear.'

Santillán settled his robe again on his shoulders; once more enjoying the thrill that raced through his fingers as they sank deep into the fur. 'I want the innkeeper to come too. Mistress, see to it that no one enters this room until I say so.'

Chapter 19

The city was already dark when the small party emerged from the inn. Warm, yellow lights pushed their way from windows and open doors across the now blackened pathway; torches in their sconces on stone-fronted buildings curling their flames and smoke above their heads, guiding them towards the Royal Chancellery; two of the guards carried lanterns at the head and two to the rear as they marched along to ensure no one left or joined the group. People stopped to wonder and gossip at the fate of the two men being escorted by the Chief Magistrate for Civil Crimes with his constables or guards.

As they progressed so the streets became wider and better lit; the houses were bigger here, mansions and small palaces, each with a torch-lit entrance for carriages or horses. Their footsteps no longer rang out loud or echoed like a small army and there was no one to witness their progress.

They suddenly turned to the right and through a yawning archway then up a short flight of stone steps and into a large room, which because of its sparse furnishings loomed even larger.

The innkeeper was ordered to wait here with two guards, the rest continued through another doorway and into an equally large room with an enormous desk and several chairs and this evening a welcoming fire in its huge hearth.

Santillán ordered the remaining guards to accompany Cristobal into an adjoining room and secure him in the cell.

Cristobal allowed himself a gentle smile. This room was so similar to the *locutorio* of the convent in Madrigal, except that behind the huge grille only a simple table, chair, and bed awaited him and not two or three black-robed Augustinian nuns.

He sat down to wait and think. Patience was all that was required. His eyes wandered over the terra cotta tiles of the floor studying the regularly interspersed white tiles with their blue stylised rabbits or cockerels. If nothing else, he decided, it was good to sit down. He must have been on his feet for hours: there was his walk to the theatre, throughout the performance, his return to the inn, all that nonsense with Imelda and the magistrate, and finally his grand march here. This all reminded him, too, that he had not eaten since about noon and he was hungry. No doubt something would be arranged as soon as the magistrate had sorted out this stupid absurdity or at least how to go about it. Cristobal's eyes lingered on the bed; that was another thing, he would insist on a mattress.

Back in the room that he had nominated as his office, Santillán placed the locket, the ring, and the letter on the desk. A young servant lad helped remove the fur-lined cloak, Santillán's fingers enjoying passing over the lining for the last time that day. His indoor robe was nowhere near as grand but it was still the robe of a Chief

Magistrate, and there were not many in this great country who could boast such an honour.

He and the servant turned his chair to the fire, allowing its warmth to rid his bones and aching belly of the cold October night.

After sending the lad to 'request' the presence of the royal silversmith Santillán leaned over the desk. He picked up the locket, looking at his secretary who had arrived with a bundle of papers under one arm and with an army of quills and ink and sand pots in his hands.

'When you have your papers ready for statements bring me my magnifying glass.' He opened the locket; she was quite a beauty, there was no denying it. Was she a nun, that could well be a wimple, but then again she might be a young widow, especially when she was wearing such a marvellous diamond and emerald necklace; what, who, was she? And the little lap dog, no clues there.

'Have the innkeeper sent in.'

The frightened man shuffled into the room. He was already overcome by the size of the building and now standing before the immense rich and dark oak desk with the Chief Magistrate larger than life behind it, and with yet another man also in black robes with pens and paper before him seated to one side of the intimidating wooden barrier he felt that he, the locket, the ring, the letter, had no business here whatsoever. A fuss about nothing that was all it was, he should never have told his wife, but it was more than his life's worth to suggest any of this now.

'Tell me what you see on my desk,' Santillán demanded.

'Like I said before, those are the things belonging to the man who had rented the room: they're his, the ring, the locket, and I reckon that's the letter.'

'Are you sure?'

'Wouldn't mistake them anywhere, your worship; the ring, what with the king on it and all; the locket with its patterns and the pretty woman inside. I'm sure that is the letter my wife found.'

When he had finished his repeated and strange story about the king and just whose master Philip was he was told to sign a piece of paper.

'I can't write but I can make my mark,' he answered the secretary proudly. He looked at the neat rows of black on the white paper and guessed they would be the words he had spoken; then he took the pen to make an upper case *P* with a flurry of horizontal lines flowing from its curve criss-crossing this way and that across the paper.

'What is your name?' asked the kindly secretary.

'Pablo, sir.'

Pablo was then printed below his mark.

Santillán read the statement and nodded, 'You may go; we know where you are if we have further need of you. No gossiping, or my guards will come for you and your wife.'

The innkeeper left the room like a man finally freed from his gaolers, and only too glad to be going home.

The servant announced the arrival of the silversmith. He stayed long enough to take his cloak, a magnificent blue woollen cloak with the badge of the Royal Guild of Silversmiths high on the left breast.

'No need for time wasting, I want your opinion on these.' Santillán pointed to the exhibits on his desk and pushed his magnifying glass in his direction.

'With respect, your worship, I never go anywhere without my own.' He searched out his lens then picked up the locket. 'Well I never, see our mark? This was made in our workshop by order of the Princess Juana, the king's sister. Oh, it was made years ago when I was but an apprentice. What an introduction to the craft; I tell you, that was something never to be forgotten.'

'Do get on with it,' Santillán's patience was always of short duration.

'Well, as I said, it was made when she was regent, so that would be in the fifties when King Philip was in England, or Flanders, or France perhaps. She lived here in Valladolid at the convent ...'

'It may have escaped you, but I was born and raised in this city. You say in the fifties, can this be verified?

'Most certainly, it will be in the books.'

'We can return to that later. I hope you will be just as successful with this other piece,' Santillán pushed the ring towards the silversmith.

'Yes, this is from our workshops, too, there's our mark,' the smith inspected the ring through his lens. It will be on our books. This was made much more recently; the Princess Isabel Clara Eugenia had it made as a gift for someone.'

'Interesting; so, it was made for our king's daughter and not so very long ago, at that. Back to the locket; tell me then if this makes any sense to you. You say it was made for Princess Juana, and we all know what she looked like and we also know she's been dead for years; God rest her soul. Open it and tell me what you see.'

'Well, well, well; I know of the lady. The artist brought these miniatures to have them fitted into the locket.'

'When was this?

'A few years since, I would have to have that checked; more than five yet less than ten. Interestingly I know of the lady, she is Her Excellency Doña Ana of Austria.'

Santillán hated being caught out like this, but he had to admit to himself that he had never heard of such a person. He looked accusingly at his secretary as if he'd been responsible for withholding this vital information, 'Should we know of her?'

The secretary could only shrug his ignorance.

'Your worship it was all hushed up,' the silversmith was quick to point out, 'right from the beginning. I knew nothing about it until the paintings arrived in our workshop. Seems she is the, what should I say; she is the illegitimate daughter of Don Juan of Austria. Hidden away in a convent very early on; anyway she's a nun at the Convent of Our Lady of Grace in Madrigal. What she'd be wanting this for, I've no idea, but that's none of my business so long as I get paid.'

'I agree, good sir,' Santillán stood up. 'You have been of great assistance.'

'And these things have ended up in your hands, lost were they?'

'As you so rightly said, provided you got paid for them then that is all that matters.'

'Could be theft, of course.'

'I insist upon discretion, especially since we are dealing with someone related, one way or another, to the royal family. You must understand that this meeting never took place. No doubt you will eventually be rewarded for your silence; the alternative I am sure you can imagine.' He called for the servant, 'See that the silversmith is attended to his home.'

Santillán mulled over the smith's information. He read the secretary's notes; toyed with the locket. 'So, secretary Mauricio, we have quite a little mystery developing here. Tell the guard to bring in the prisoner.'

Cristobal was conducted into the room to stand before the magistrate.

Santillán leaned his forearms on the desk. 'The time has come for you to give some answers.'

'Gladly, your worship, if it is in my power to do so.'

'Do not irritate me.' He turned the open locket towards Cristobal. 'I understand that this young lady is Her Excellency Doña Ana of Austria, the daughter of Don Juan who was half brother to the king.'

'That is correct.'

'How come you have it in your possession?'

'It is a gift because I had been the *pastelero* in her ladyship's service for some time; at the convent in Madrigal.'

'Is she a nun?'

'Doña Ana has taken the veil, but she does have her own apartments and she maintains a small household.'

'This ring, how did you come by it?'

'Doña Ana thought it would keep me safe wherever I travelled, bearing the king's likeness, and I am sure it would have done so had I not been so stupid. I have no wish to embarrass my lady but if you were to make discreet enquiries you will find everything I have said to be true.'

'There is no need for you to tell me my job,' Santillán yelled at him. 'Now we come to the letter.'

'I am not at liberty to divulge ...'

'You exhaust my patience. Well, pastry cook, you may not be at liberty, but I am, as an agent of the crown. Does it not seem strange to you that there should be no name on the front of this letter; or is that you know the receiver's identity?

Santillán took his dagger and sliced under the seal. He read, *'My lord, my life, how I suffer in your absence. Although for everyone else the days may be short for me they are an eternity. I have to constantly remind myself of Sister Isabel and her advice to remain patient. I pray to God that He protects you, my king and master.'* He laid the letter down slowly and with exaggerated precision, placed his elbows on the arms of his chair before linking his fingers across his corpulence. He searched the *pastelero*'s face for a clue. There was nothing.

'Who wrote this letter and who is it for?'

'I am not at liberty to divulge ...'

'God give me strength! Sadly for you señor — what did you say your name is?'

'I did not, your worship.'

'Well, sadly for you, you will remain in my custody until I have received satisfactory information from this Doña Ana regarding the jewellery and this somewhat intimate letter.'

The expression on Cristobal's face never altered; there was no sign of embarrassment, guilt, fear, consternation, agitation.

'Take him back to the cell.'

'A word, your worship?' Cristobal paused, 'I have money enough to pay therefore I would like a mattress for my bed, and I would certainly appreciate a decent dinner and a jar of wine.'

Santillán knew the man was within his rights; after all he hadn't been charged with anything, he actually wasn't a prisoner, and strangely he wasn't even objecting to being put behind bars. Nevertheless he had to be put in his place. 'You speak too hastily taking the words from my mouth. I would remind you of two things: first, food and bedding lie solely within my jurisdiction; secondly, and far more important, you must beware of annoying me.'

Cristobal bowed and was led away.

'Mauricio, write a letter to this Doña Ana, to the effect that I have detained someone who says he was her *pastelero*. He has amongst his possessions a number of items of jewellery which he insists she gave him and that I await her instructions. Once that it is done I think we shall have a glass of wine.'

He walked to the fireplace and stepped onto the stone flagged hearth, before resting his brow and hands against the warm bricks. After a few moments of quiet contemplation gazing at the crackling logs he decided to share his thoughts with his secretary, 'You know; I put my success down to industry and lack of greed, always esteeming honour rather than wealth; and that is the truth, as God is my maker. I would say I have been steadfast in applying myself to my official duties by day, and never negligent in personally patrolling the city by night; I think you must agree with me on that too. I shall approach this latest business: a strange man purporting to be a tradesman but speaking more like a nobleman, a royal lady, jewels, and love letters; a business which can be nothing less than an affair of state; I shall approach it with the same dedication and discretion; once resolved I will share the resulting triumph in the same modest manner but this time with you, my secretary, for you are all—important to me.

Chapter 20

Two days later found Santillán at his desk writing or, to be exact, meticulously copying in his finest hand ... *I have to constantly remind myself of Sister Isabel and to remain patient* ... do sit down Mauricio, I shall be with you soon ... *I pray that God protects you, my king and master*. There now, that is ready. He put it with the one he had copied earlier. 'What have you there, Mauricio?

'Nothing more than a waste of your valuable time and certainly an unacceptable waste of good ink and paper, so far as I can see. This comes from a horde of common folk crowding at the door insisting that they witnessed the excellent horsemanship of this Cristobal fellow and having seen the jewels at the inn or at others in the city where apparently he was forever flaunting them. Others claim to have been his friend up to that very moment when they saw the jewels, before making themselves scarce because they realised he was a thief. They all came here seeking rewards no doubt. Anyway I have made notes of their statements.'

'I expect that the damned innkeeper or his wife found it too difficult to keep quiet. No matter.'

A servant entered, 'Don Pedro de Tapias has arrived; he says it is a matter of some urgency and must see you, your worship.'

'Send him in; good to have a like mind here with me,' he twiddled with the quill in his fingers. 'Mauricio, lock these letters with everything else relating to this case.' They were placed carefully in the leather document wallet and handed to the secretary.

An elderly and extremely thin soul with unkempt grey hair reaching down to the ruff of his judge's robes removed his gloves and rubbed his hands.

'I know, I know,' he whined at Santillán, 'and October has just begun.'

'Be my guest Pedro; rid yourself of the cold at the fire. To what do I owe the honour?'

'I received the strangest letter this morning from Doña Ana de Austria, she sounds most distraught. I guess she must be feeling so in order to write to me regarding a person and something about which I know nothing. I have met her on one or two occasions, obviously, coming as I do from Madrigal, but this is most odd, most extraordinary,' he handed over the letter.

'*I beg you; tell them they must never, ever, torture the prisoner. Despite his appearance they are dealing with a knight, a cavalier of some importance ...*' Santillán nodded, 'and so my suspicions grow. Read this; a lady with some temper. This is a copy, the original is safely locked away.'

De Tapias read Ana's angry response to her servant's detention, 'This does surprise me, I had always considered her to be of a quiet nature, although unhappy she always seemed to be making the best of things; I don't think she takes very kindly to being a nun.'

'I had already decided against giving this man his liberty, despite the lady's fury. There was something bothering me.'

He brought the *pastelero*'s belongings from the cupboard and displayed them on the desk, indicating the cup, the spoon, the dish, the table ware, all brought from the inn. De Tapias responded with a shrug and a non-committal questioning arch of the eyebrows.

Santillán continued, 'So the man was telling the truth, they had been given him by his employer. Nothing unusual about that we would say. The anger of the employer emphasises his innocence. However I have kept him, and this,' he put the note on the desk, 'convinces me I am right. Now, is this anger or panic on the lady's part?'

'Most odd, certainly; in one letter she refers to him as her servant, her pastry chef, while in the other she states he is a gentleman of some rank.'

'The whole business is curious, read this.'

De Tapias scratched through his cap at his grizzled head as he read Ana's words to *my life and my lord.*

'You see, Pedro, your reluctant nun is in love! Now, the question is, is she in love with this *pastelero* fellow, or is he a messenger for someone else?'

De Tapias took off his cap in desperation and rummaged through his shock of hair causing Santillán to gather his robes more tightly about him, 'You should have some of that stack removed, a regular breeding ground if you ask me. I know we all suffer from time to time but you are positively encouraging the little devils. Take our lord the king as a prime example; a short trimmed beard and very short hair.'

De Tapias snorted, 'Very short indeed, but then the man is almost bald!'

'Is that anyway to speak of our paymaster?'

'Be that as it may, my barber keeps a close check.'

'Come and meet my prisoner.' Santillán led the way.

The moment the two judges entered the room the guard stood to attention and Cristobal rose hastily hoping for some positive news.

'This is the magistrate de Tapias, señor ... '

'A humble pastry cook, your worship,' he turned to Santillán, 'has any word arrived from Madrigal?'

'Nothing,' Santillán cleared his throat of the lie. 'Now, the other day when you went to the theatre; perhaps you can give us more information?'

'I went to see one of Rueda's plays. It started well enough with gods and goddesses descending from the mountains on to the stage, but I heard not a word, those on stools and benches in front of the stage were restless only waiting for the comedy parts, you know those scenes with the doctor and his servants and their racy language, so I heard nothing.'

'Thank the heavens for small mercies. And you were not talking or listening to someone next to you, perhaps?'

'No, I knew no one there. Once the ruffians began to fight I thought it best to leave.'

'Where did you spend the time before returning to the inn?'

Cristobal smiled at the questions, 'I understood that I was only to be held while you awaited word from Madrigal? This appears to be an interrogation. I stopped at an inn, took my wine into the patio area and watched some gentlemen with cards or dice.'

'When you were there did you chance to speak to anyone?

'I neither spoke nor met anyone. Following my drink I made my way to my inn where I met your worship.'

Santillán tried a final parting shot, 'My friend here often visits Madrigal. It was where he was born and raised.'

The eagerly awaited change of expression or altered countenance failed to appear. Santillán beckoned de Tapias to follow him from the room.

Chapter 21

'Hmm, dress and speech, neither are those of a common tradesman,' de Tapias stroked at his beard as they made their way towards the fire.

'Precisely! Servant, my friend and I will partake of a small chocolate.'

'My goodness, what an unexpected treat!'

'Sir,' Mauricio scurried in, 'one of your constables has delivered these. A messenger was intercepted at the inn. Someone had given the man the address of the *pastelero*; I have him held below. Here are the two letters he expected to deliver.

'Good, good, well off you go to make your report.' He chanced a smile, 'I wonder if either of these will be the missing piece in my puzzle.'

He turned away to stoop slightly, clutching at his stomach.

'Still bothering you, then?

'Nothing but a few drops of hot chocolate and my daily medicine can't put to rights. And here it is. Pour for the magistrate and me then set the pot near the fire.'

The chocolate was stirred then poured, its glutinous brown mass emerging from the long spout of the coffee pot along with steam and a fantastic aroma.

Santillán took a small glass of rose water from a small chest to add a few grains of Mastiche which he swallowed with a bitter grimace before reaching for his beloved chocolate.

De Tapias turned his bowl in his hands enjoying its comforting warmth then sipped at the luxurious drink allowing its slippery smoothness flood his mouth and throat. This morning was proving to be far better than he ever could have imagined.

They sat quietly enjoying the moment, each deep in thought.

'Have the rest,' Santillán rubbed comfortingly across his stomach inducing a glorious belch of relief, 'That feels better.'

'You should take life more slowly, my friend,' mumbled de Tapias stirring the dregs of chocolate before draining the pot.

'Soon, perhaps soon; but the letters. I think the one in a lady's hand. *My lord and life, no one knows better than me that my faith burns as brightly as ever it did. Just because I am faced with amorous exploits does not mean it will burn any the less. May God guard you my lord and my consolation.*' There can surely be no doubting, then, that the lady is in love with the pastry chef?'

'All things are possible. Remember she was just a child when she entered the convent. I feel she is an unhappy nun who finally met a handsome stranger.'

'Perhaps you, too, have visited the theatre more than is good for you. Suppose our mysterious servant is simply the messenger?'

'You worry too much, my friend, or are you enjoying yourself?'

'I know this much, I will not let go until I have solved it, despite the old stomach.'

Santillán scanned the second letter, this one in a man's hand, 'My God! The plot thickens and yet becomes clearer. Listen to this: *Sire, my king, your note has brought renewed life to my lady and to us your servants ... she has been melancholic the last few days ... the little girl, Clara Eugenia, is well ... her nursemaid brings her almost every day ... Poderos has brought some excellent outfits for our child ... my lady dresses her entirely, all the way from under-linens to ruffs. My king ...* did you hear that? *My king, my lady has decided it best to close the pastry shop and house and have the nursemaid and child removed to Salamanca. Men will arrive in disguise, perhaps as servants of that Blomberg woman, to take them away ... your humble servant, Miguel.*'

'May I see the letter?' De Tapias read its contents rather more carefully, 'Well I never, the old rascal rears his head again after all these years,' he handed the letter back to finish his chocolate, scraping his finger into the bowl and licking it clean, something as good as this was not to be wasted on stupid letters, then he continued, 'Miguel de los Santos arrived at Madrigal years ago as its vicar following the directives of King Philip II. At one time he had been exiled from Portugal in the early eighties because of his support for Don Antonio ...'

'So, his support has been rekindled. My friend, I now know who our pastry chef is - he is Don Antonio. He wears the ring she gave him for good luck, he wears the locket. He will take the throne of Portugal with Doña Ana as his queen … '

'Calm down. First I must remind you that Don Antonio, far from ever becoming the king of Portugal, is far from being a lover - he'll be in his sixties by now. That man through there is certainly not that old.'

'If not Antonio, and I think he is, then he is a messenger for him. We have stumbled upon a treasonable conspiracy, a very serious situation demanding action. I must inform the king of this treachery.'

'Should this be true, then I would suggest or even remind you that more judges will be necessary to deal with this case if indeed the situation is at this level.'

'I shall copy these and set out with all my copies to the Escorial. News will have travelled to Madrigal already that the letters have been intercepted; I shall send for my brother Diego. He can conduct our pastry fellow to Madrigal and hold him until I return with his majesty's instructions. In the meantime you will get that hair cut and generally tidy yourself up and get to Madrigal to await me. Needless to say you will not visit the convent nor talk to nuns or priests.'

Santillán walked to and fro caressing his bulging front before going to the other room to deliver his decision regarding further questioning.

On his return he suddenly stopped, a crease of doubt furrowing his brow. Had he spoken to the pastry chef while they were both standing, or had he knelt? Did he allow the chef to remain seated while he stood, as becomes the lowly born in the presence of a king? Had he done the latter then he would have publicly acknowledged him. Dear God, if only his stomach would settle. An extra potion of Mastiche was called for, he took a handkerchief and mopped at the sweat on his brow.

Chapter 22

On the day following Santillán's submission of all those immaculate copies of letters, statements, and reports detailing the development of the eventual trial in Valladolid, each one written in his own 'fair hand', he was commanded to attend King Philip's court.

He and Mauricio travelled the last part of their journey from the small nearby town of El Escorial where the local hosts had been more than generous with their time and attention.

Their mules, mused Santillán miserably, slowly and daintily picked their way along the stony road bringing them ever closer to their masters' destiny.

The huge Escorial: part palace, part Jeronymite Monastery, part mausoleum for Philip's family, focused Santillán's thoughts on images of heaps of cold stones; austere, dry, melancholic – a reflection of the king himself, like as not – but impressive nonetheless, a remarkable building; so much having been completed in just twenty years or so.

They were met at the entrance and conducted to the throne room by guards whose boots clanged their military authority at every step along the corridors.

Santillán's resolve was disappearing fast, increasing doubts and uncertainties taking its place.

Why had he written to the king, not once but twice, insisting on full powers of investigation? He had, he reminded himself, because it was a civil case and he was, after all, a fully robed judge of civil cases!

The throne room was long, expansive and chilly. Santillán had by now quite changed his mind about the dry, cold, Escorial stones of the Escorial. They were more than likely damp; he had a nose for two things, dampness and intrigue.

There were people, lots of people, and quite possibly, their situations were all similar to his; all summoned here to the king's side to answer probing questions.

Braziers were in abundance and there were two fireplaces but there was still little cheer to be had. On the left hand side of the room stood the curved back throne looking totally inadequate swamped as it was by the expanse of the carpeted dais and the unnecessarily huge royal canopy. Several tapestries and paintings helped to disguise the blue, cold, half-tiled walls completing the picture.

Santillán concluded that the pastry chef was no common thief. Damn! Why did that thought have to rear its ugly head just at this moment? He must try to keep his mind clear, ready for any query that he knew the king was certainly determined to thrust at him.

He approached the dais and bowed, only to be summarily dismissed by the king. A daring, hasty glance towards his majesty showed a thin, white, and emaciated figure, with swollen knees on legs that had appeared, miraculously unaided, from thigh boots far too wide to support anything so meagre. Why no one had suggested that he ought to wear a longer and fuller cloak to disguise his weaknesses, greatly surprised Santillán. On the other hand Patias would have been impressed by the sparse and short white hair on his majesty's head. Dear Lord, but those ice-cold eyes could penetrate the wilderness between king and courtiers. Philip's right hand was heavily bandaged, and surely there was a most objectionable, if not putrescent, smell emanating from that area.

Santillán and Mauricio moved slowly away.

A young woman, past her prime, stood a few feet away from the king; she was most definitely the Princess Isabel Clara Eugenia, looking completely lonely and isolated. Quivering pearls tumbled from her tiny jewelled bonnet, cascading over her hair and on to her forehead. Her satin dress was awash with even more pearls and gems creating such a show. This was more like it, Santillán congratulated himself, and this was the way to keep oneself occupied, to keep oneself free from 'what ifs'.

'I hear she misses her sister,' Mauricio whispered.

'She must, they were so close, and barely a year's difference in their ages.'

'I understand it should not be too long before she gets married and moves to Flanders, with the Archduke Albert.'

'I doubt Philip would allow her to leave, she is too good as his private secretary.'

'I'm surprised he would even consider her as such; let's face it, the world of politics and business is not the place for a woman. And if he truly had trust in her, why should she not inherit?'

Mauricio smiled up at Rodrigo, 'We are becoming far too serious. Why not concentrate our attention on the young Prince Philip?'

The rotund, fat-cheeked, and red-lipped sixteen year old had demonstrated for some time a total lack of interest in all things governmental, preferring to leave that boring aspect of life for lesser mortals. He stood on the dais beaming his satisfaction at the joyous life style of princes; light hearted past times and a virtual mania for all things religious.

'He looks the very epitome of everything that is said about him,' Santillán commented as his stroll involuntarily lengthened to a stride and he tapped his hands nervously together behind his back.

'You are worried, sir.'

'Yes, quite, because I am quite out of my depth here, too many clever men.'

'But there can be few more astute than you, your worship.'

'Bless you, Mauricio; you do me the power of good.'

'Everything will work out, sir.'

'If only we were in my comfortable Valladolid. Have I done the right thing?'

'You had no choice. Her Excellency, Doña Ana, the half-niece of King Philip, is obviously deeply involved. You are more than likely to be asked to conduct an enquiry into treason; and, I might add, there is no one better than you to offer such a case the honour and justice it warrants.'

'What would I do without you,' Santillán clapped his secretary's back.

A dreaded hush descended on the throne room. Judge Santillán could scarcely breathe; his stomach reacted wildly, an iron claw or fist relentlessly tearing at it. The time had come. Moura, King Philip's trusted Portuguese secretary, the proven arch master of bribery and corruption, followed by the Inquisitor Llanos had mounted the two steps to the dais to take up their positions next to the king.

Santillán was told to approach.

Philip's voice knifed the air, 'This is Llanos de Valdes. I have nominated him the Judge Apostolic in this case, because when all else fails in bringing a persecution to a successful result, I always revert to heresy; nothing competes with the church being put in jeopardy. But there is always treason, and this is your area, Santillán.'

'I am honoured, your majesty.'

'The court is dismissed. I need to speak in private with Don Rodrigo Santillán.' King Philip rushed into his speech, 'Judge, this is a most serious business; all avenues must be explored, there can be no loopholes or means of escape. You must understand that this is another reason for my calling in Llanos; it is not because of my having any doubts on your behalf.'

Santillán nodded thinking, so the king is still afraid. Obviously there are still enemies to be silenced, and there continues the country's suffering year upon year of drought, pestilence, famine, financial disaster.

'With permission, your majesty, I would prefer to conduct the enquiry on my own. And I do see problems arising when the Church is allowed to administer torture to gain a confession, but civil law demands the prisoner be charged first; this is anything but equitable.'

'On the other hand magistrate with your abilities this whole vexed issue could be cleared up in no time at all, needing no other than your good self to bring about an acceptable conclusion for all concerned. I admit to being impressed with your report.' A royal frosted smile was set free for the merest of moments. 'So, you may proceed.' Philip turned as if to leave.

Mauricio was desperately trying to catch every nuance of every spoken word, furiously scribbling them down with his charcoal stick, on one after another sheet of virgin paper. And still Santillán was not content, 'Your majesty, may I be allowed just one further question?' He was desperate to have every aspect of this case ordered in his mind before embarking on his task.

'When I am addressing this prisoner, who may or may not be above my station, whether buffoon or traitor, do I sit or stand before him, or do we both stand or sit?'

Santillán had gone too far, Philip was not amused. If only it were possible for him to bring back and swallow all those lamentable words. He started to sweat, a foul, acrid sweat coursing from his armpits and into his beloved robe; the job he had so earnestly sought was most likely lost for good along with his career, his status, his freedom, his pension. But no, another smile had appeared, or was it a leer; a sneer perhaps?

'Magistrate, we are talking treason here; who cares who is sitting or standing? In any case, you are the judge. Moura; take over would you, let us not delay, even minutes may prove essential to our success.' Philip was growing agitated; he sat down and began to comfort his aching temples.

'Santillán,' Moura began, 'the king believes that this to be most decidedly treason; all the more so since the introduction of that little girl, *at last, as such a mother of such a child, and a child of such a mother* as Miguel de los Santos so eloquently puts it. And one must ask why the child is called Clara Eugenia. Most suspicious; what does it mean?'

Princess Isabel could not resist smiling and shaking her head in Moura's direction; surely it was all far too silly for words. It would pass soon enough.

'One might have thought that with Antonio Crato out of the way with a price on his head, the Braganza family well and truly bought off, and the successful annexation of Portugal since fifteen eighty, there would be no trouble; and there hasn't been until this Miguel and the *pastelero* problem. Judge, you caught the whole nasty business before it had a chance to grow; Miguel, *pastelero*, and Her Excellency Doña Ana, are plotting to usurp the Portuguese throne,' he beckoned Santillán closer to whisper, 'I assume there is no need to remind you that every detail of your investigation will be reported back to his majesty, and that you must never enact any new line of questioning or move progress without his permission.'

Epilogue

The author Linda Carlino, my beloved wife, finished these chapters on January 3, 2010. She had neither the mental nor physical strength to continue writing. She passed away, quietly and peacefully, eleven days later.
She had fought against illness, courageously and without complaining, for a year. But she had had enough and is now at rest and peaceful.

Charles Carlino

Historical Note

King Sebastian I of Portugal disappeared in battle in Morocco in August 1578. His disappearance was never satisfactorily accounted for nor were any remains ever positively identified as his.

Gabriel de Espinosa, known as the Pastry Chef of Madrigal (El Pastelero de Madrigal) bore a surprising resemblance to the king. He posed as the king and had many supporters.

Espinosa was convicted of conspiracy and sentenced in 1595. He was hanged, beheaded and quartered and his remains were displayed at the entrances to the town of Madrigal. A fellow conspirator was hanged in the Plaza Mayor of Madrid.

Ana of Austria (Doña María Ana de Austria) was deprived of her privileges and detained in strict confinement in the Convent of Our Lady of Grace in Avila.

Three years later she was pardoned and moved to the convent Monasterio de Santa María la Real de Las Huelgas in Burgos where she eventually became abbess.

also by
Linda Carlino

That Other Juana
Queen Juana I of Spain
(Juana la Loca)

*A story of obsessive love, uncontrolled passion
- and cruel, cynical betrayal.*

A Matter of Pride
Charles V, (Holy Roman Emperor)

*An historical novel that takes a humorous and
rather sceptical view of Charles V (HRE) the
king, soldier and lover – a story of power,
passion and regrets.*

Wives & Other Women
(Philip II of Spain)

*This is the story of Philip seeking a suitable
male heir in loveless marriages –
and his compulsive pursuit of other women.*

VeritasPublishing

For information about the publisher, future publishing plans, and how to purchase books:

www.VeritasPublishing.co.uk

The Author

For information about the author:

www.LindaCarlino.com

To contact the author, ask questions, or comment:

LindaCarlino@VeritasPublishing.co.uk
or
author@LindaCarlino.com

www.ingramcontent.com/pod-product-compliance
Lightning Source LLC
Chambersburg PA
CBHW071631140626
46555CB00022B/2214

* 9 7 8 0 9 5 5 5 9 8 0 3 6 *